TRUE DETECTIVE STORIES

Fascinating, frightening or just plain frustrating? These eight gripping stories show detective work as it really is—and sometimes truth is stranger than fiction. Read about the ghostly dream that helped to solve a baffling murder mystery, some clever detectives' tricks that led to the conviction of the 'Laurel and Hardy' jewel thieves, and the crafty blackmailer who nearly got away with the perfect crime. With facts on fingerprinting, police files and the Flying Squad, *True Detective Stories* brings you face to face with real-life detectives, and some sinister cases it is their job to solve.

TRUE DETECTIVE STORIES

Terry Deary

Illustrated by David Wyatt

Galaxy

CHIVERS PRESS
BATH

First published 1996
by
Scholastic Children's Books
This Large Print edition published by
Chivers Press
by arrangement with
Scholastic Children's Books
2000

ISBN 0 7540 6126 4

British Library Cataloguing in Publication Data

Deary, Terry
  True detective stories.—Large print ed.
  1. Crime—Juvenile literature   2. Criminal investigation—
  Juvenile literature   3. Large type books
  I. Title
  363.2'5

ISBN 0-7540-6126-4

Printed and bound in Great Britain by
REDWOOD BOOKS, Trowbridge, Wiltshire

For Rosemary Bromley, who deserves
more than 10% of the credit

CONTENTS

INTRODUCTION

Sherlock Holmes never solved a mystery.

Hercule Poirot never cracked a crime.

Columbo never caught a crook.

Miss Marple never unmasked a murderer.

Why not? Because they, and a hundred other famous detectives, are all characters invented by writers. Detective stories are great fun. They are puzzles for you to solve, they are exciting adventures to enjoy, they are crimes to chill you and mysteries to entertain you. But if you're ever the victim of a real crime it's no use looking for one of these clever detectives in the *Yellow Pages*. You'll have to call the local police and have it investigated by a real detective.

The work of a real detective is rather different from that shown in books, films and television programmes. Not many people know the names of these real detectives the way they know the name of Sherlock Holmes. And not many people know their true stories.

Here is a collection of stories about

2

real crime-crackers who have solved puzzles just as interesting as those investigated by heroes in books. Stories that are just as curious, chilling, mysterious and entertaining; stories from around the world from Australia to Britain; stories about police detectives . . . as well as some about amateur investigators who never expected to be solving a crime.

Some of the words spoken by the characters have been invented to make them easier to read as stories, but the cases are true and they were solved by real detectives. As well as the stories there are fact files to help you understand how crime investigators worked in the past and how they work now.

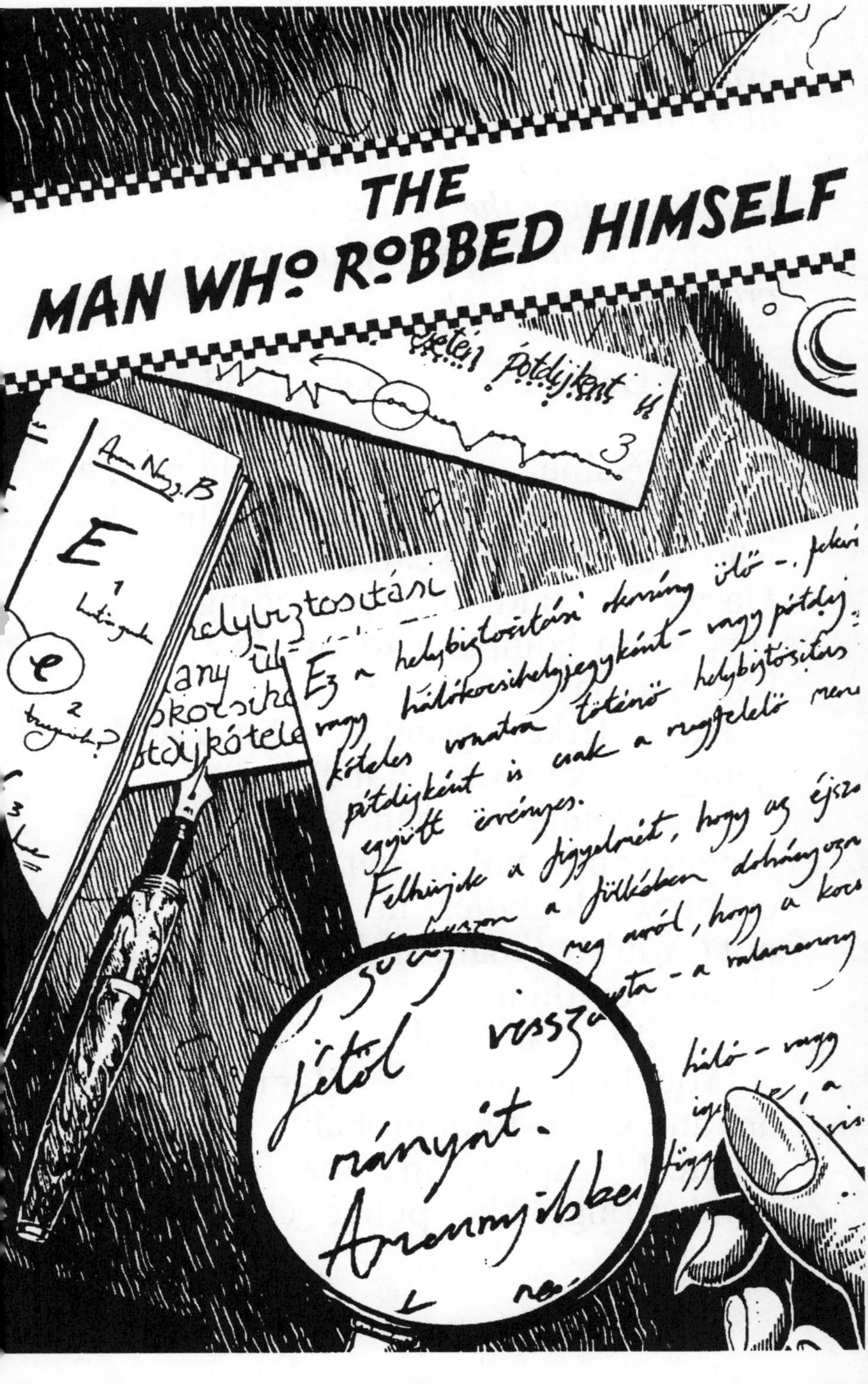
THE
MAN WHO ROBBED HIMSELF

Police sometimes call on the help of experts to catch criminals. An expert can also produce evidence which will prove a suspect is not to blame. But what happens when the police and the expert disagree? Can the expert turn detective to prove his case?

Budapest, Hungary, 1938

Hanna Sulner sat down heavily at the restaurant table and looked at the man who was already seated there. 'Sorry, Hary,' she said, 'I'm not going to be very good company today. I've had a bad, bad day.'

Hary Erkel grinned. 'So, you're going to take it out on me, yes?'

The young woman stuck out her tongue and pulled her straight dark eyebrows together in a scowl. 'Why not? You're a man, and men think they know everything.'

'We do,' Hary said.

'You know *nothing*,' Hanna said. 'I am an expert. I am probably Hungary's greatest expert in the study of handwriting. The police call for my

6

help a dozen times. But *this* time, when I give my opinion, they ignore me. They arrest an innocent man, destroy his wife's life and practically tell me I am a fool or a liar. Well, I am not mistaken. I just wish I knew how to prove it,' she said.

'Who is this innocent man and what did he do?' Hary asked gently.

'He did nothing! That's what I'm telling you!' Hanna replied. One or two of the customers in the restaurant looked up from their meals to see what she was so agitated about. She lowered her voice. 'His name is Miklos and he is accused of theft. He is the accountant for a small business in Budapest and he is paid 1000 forints a month. When he left work on the Friday evening before Christmas there were half a million forints in the safe. When he returned after Christmas the safe was empty.'

'How was the safe opened?' Hary asked.

'It had been opened by someone who knew the combination lock numbers. And only two people knew those numbers: Miklos and the owner.

7

There was only one set of fingerprints on the safe—'

'Don't tell me,' Hary cut in. 'They belonged to Miklos.'

'They did,' Hanna said.

'That's what they call an open and shut case,' Hary shrugged.

The young woman glared at him again. 'Typical man, jumping to conclusions!' she hissed. 'The police didn't think they had enough evidence to arrest him. They made enquiries at the Budapest banks and made an important discovery. On the Monday after the robbery a woman had paid nearly half a million forints into a bank account. She used the name Anna Nagy.'

'A common enough name,' Hary said.

'Unfortunately it was the name of Miklos's wife before she married him,' Hanna said.

Hary thought carefully, in case he irritated the handwriting expert any more. 'The police supposed he'd given the money to his wife and she'd paid it into a bank, then?'

'They did,' Hanna agreed. 'And, to make things worse, they went around to Miklos's house and discovered they'd bought a lot of new things for Christmas: a new radio, a pram for the baby Anna was expecting, new furniture for the nursery and so on. They found receipts for 7,000 forints.'

'It looks bad for Miklos,' Hary muttered.

'The poor man had saved it! For four years, he'd been saving. Then they had a spending spree so they were all ready for the arrival of their first baby.'

Hary picked up a menu and studied it. 'You have to admit it looks a bit unlikely. The police have arrested people on less evidence than that.'

Hanna nodded miserably. 'Just soup for me. I'm not very hungry.'

'This case has really upset you, hasn't it?' Hary said.

'Yes,' she said, twisting the table napkin miserably. 'Miklos has had the most amazing bad luck. There were just two people who could prove that his wife hadn't paid that money into the bank, and one of those people was the bank cashier, of course. There was every chance that he would remember what the mysterious Anna Nagy looked like and tell the police that it wasn't Miklos's wife.'

'Don't tell me,' Hary said. 'He'd forgotten all about Anna Nagy.'

'Worse,' Hanna said. 'He'd suffered a heart attack at Christmas and died.'

'That is bad luck,' Hary agreed. 'So who was the other person who could prove Miklos's wife didn't make that payment?'

Hanna looked up. 'Why, *me* of course. They had the paying-in slip for that half-million forints. It was signed "Anna Nagy". The police asked Miklos's wife to sign that name, then they gave both specimens to me to compare.'

'Don't tell me. They were the same. His wife had done the robbery without telling him!' Hary laughed.

Hanna snapped, 'Now you're being silly.'

'Sorry,' the young man said. 'Tell me about it.'

'The   signatures   were   totally

different. A blind person could see they were not written by the same person. They didn't need *me* to tell them that.'

'But you did,' Hary put in.

'But I did. The police didn't believe me . . . they didn't want to believe me. They said she had disguised her handwriting in case she was caught. Practically called me a liar. They pressed ahead with the charge and Miklos went to court yesterday.'

Hary ordered the meal from a waiter and sat back in his chair. 'They didn't call you as a witness, then?'

'The police didn't, but Miklos's lawyer did. I was able to tell them that the person who wrote that signature was a lot older than Miklos's wife. I was also able to tell them that she had some sort of physical problem with her writing, something that made writing difficult.'

'But the court didn't believe you either?' Hary asked.

Hanna spread the napkin on her lap then crumpled it again. 'The police had an answer for that. They said that

11

Miklos's wife would be agitated when she wrote it . . . nervous about trying to cash in on her husband's crime. They also said they had checked on all the women in Budapest who are registered under the name of Anna Nagy—there were seven of them. They even put an advert in the newspapers for any other Anna Nagys to come forward if they had paid that money in legally. No one did.'

Hary Erkel was fond of Hanna and didn't want to upset her. He didn't tell her what he was really thinking—that her kind heart was trying to see the good in the accountant and wouldn't admit that he was in fact a thief. 'Your only hope would be if there was an Anna Nagy who was in Budapest and was not registered.'

'It's possible,' the young woman said shortly.

'And if this Anna Nagy didn't read the papers,' he added.

'That's possible too,' she said defiantly.

'And if this Anna Nagy hasn't been back to the bank to touch any of that money?'

'Look, I saw his wife this morning,' Hanna argued. 'She's distracted! The baby's been born to a father who's in jail for theft. She's ill with worry.'

Hary clicked his fingers. 'Hey! Have you thought about that? You said the Anna Nagy who signed the bank slip had a physical problem. Could she have been ill?'

Hanna pulled a copy of the signature from her handbag and laid it flat on the tablecloth. She traced the shaking letters with her finger. 'Yes, definitely, I should say.'

'So have you checked the hospitals? Maybe someone came into Budapest from outside—someone who isn't registered here—and paid the money into the bank, then went to hospital for some reason.'

Hanna's eyes widened. 'Why didn't I think of that?' she whispered. 'There are only four major hospitals in Budapest. I'll check them now.' She jumped to her feet so quickly the white napkin fluttered to the floor.

'But your soup!' Hary cried.

Hanna didn't hear him. She was already out of the restaurant door and hurrying down the snow-dusted street.

*   *   *

The first hospital that Hanna tried raised her hopes cruelly. She was shown into a ward where an Anna Nagy lay in bed. The young Anna smiled at Hanna and showed her the twin babies proudly. 'Yes, I am registered in Budapest and the police have already asked me about the bank account. Sorry . . . it's nothing to do with me. Best of luck,' she said.

At the second hospital there was no Anna Nagy, but at the third the receptionist checked the list of names and said, 'Yes, Ward 9. An old lady from Debrecen near the Romanian border.'

'Will she see me?' Hanna said eagerly.

'Hah!' the receptionist snorted. 'She'll see you, but she won't see you very well. She's nearly blind! She came to Budapest for an eye operation.

14

Seems she's been saving for years to have it done. By all means go and have a chat with her. Second ward on the left, third bed on the right.'

Hanna's heels clattered on the cold tile floors as she hurried towards Ward 9. The old woman in the third bed on the right seemed to be asleep. As Hanna sat in the wooden chair by the bedside it creaked and old Anna stirred.

'Is that you, nurse?'

'No. Mrs Nagy?'

'That's me.'

'My name's Hanna Sulner. I'm from the university. I wondered if you could help me by answering a few questions?'

'I'll try. Just pass me that pair of spectacles, would you?' she said. 'They don't help much yet but my eyes are getting better every day thanks to the doctors here. I'll be able to read again soon.'

'Mrs Nagy,' Hanna said as she passed the old woman the heavy glasses, 'did you bring much money with you from Debrecen?'

'Nearly half a million forints,' she

replied, squinting through the glasses at the young woman.

'And you paid it into the National Bank on Bartok Street?'

'As soon as I arrived in Budapest,' the old woman said.

'And that was when?'

'On Christmas Eve.'

Hanna struggled to keep the tremble of excitement from her voice. 'Mrs Nagy, I'll explain everything to you in a moment, but could I ask you to do just one thing for me? Would you sign your name on this blank slip of paper?'

*   *   *

'The signatures matched, of course,' Hary Erkel said a week later. They were sitting in the same restaurant.

'Of course,' Hanna said happily.

'You were right and the police were wrong.'

'Of course. What else could you expect from a bunch of simple men?' she asked wickedly.

Hary looked a little hurt. 'I seem to remember it was a simple man who gave you the idea of checking the hospitals for Anna Nagy.'

Hanna Sulner was enjoying her meal this time. Her appetite had returned. 'Some men are a little less stupid,' she admitted, 'but you don't get much more stupid than the police.'

'They've released Miklos, haven't they?' he asked.

'That's not good enough,' Hanna said. 'They only released him because some of the evidence was weakened by finding the real Mrs Nagy. Miklos could still have stolen that money— people would still have suspected him. Mud sticks. The police had to find out who did steal the cash.'

17

'So what is the answer?' Hary asked.

'Work it out for yourself,' Hanna said playfully as she tore a piece from her bread roll and chewed it.

Hary dabbed at his mouth with the napkin to buy some time. Then a corner of his mouth turned up in a smile. It spread to his eyes. 'Only two people knew the combination to the safe: Miklos and his boss. If Miklos didn't steal the money, then it must have been his boss!'

'That's what I told the police,' Hanna said.

'You—'

'And they arrested Miklos's boss last night. He admitted everything. He crept back into the office over that Christmas weekend. He wore gloves so he left no fingerprints. He opened the safe and took out the half-million forints. 'Then he claimed on the insurance and the insurance company paid him the half-million he said he'd lost!'

Hary gave a soft whistle. 'He made a cool million forints by robbing himself! Miklos was lucky he had you on the case.'

'No,' Hanna frowned. 'Miklos was very *unlucky*. Unlucky that his wife was born Anna Nagy, unlucky that the bank clerk died before the police could question him and unlucky that he chose to spend his savings at just the wrong time. Even the police might have solved the case quicker if it hadn't been for Miklos's bad luck.'

'Or if they'd had you on the police force. You'd make a brilliant detective. Ever thought of joining the force?'

Hanna raised her glass of wine and sipped it. 'Why should I?' she said and her eyes sparkled like the bubbling wine. 'I'm already a brilliant hand-writing expert . . . for a woman.'

FACT FILE

Fingerprints—FACT FILE

The police forces of the world rely heavily on experts to help with their detective work. Sometimes the experts are employed just when they are needed—doctors, for example. Others are employed as full-time policemen and women—fingerprint specialists or photographers.

Detectives can track down suspects but it is often the experts whose evidence leads to an arrest and a court conviction.

1. Fingerprints, those patterns of ridges on the tips of human fingers, are different for

21

every human being. Even identical twins have different fingerprints.

2. Detectives always hope to find a fingerprint at the scene of a crime; if they can match it to the finger pattern of a suspect then they can prove that person was there, even if the criminal says he or she wasn't.

3. Fingerprints last for life or even longer. Egyptian mummies have fingerprints and they are 3,000 years old!

4. If the fingerprints are burned or rubbed off, the same pattern of prints will grow back. In 1934, the American gangster John Dillinger paid doctors to perform plastic surgery on his fingertips. It failed. Friends suggested he dip his fingers in acid. This worked

for a while, but by the time he was caught the patterns reappeared. Another gangster, Robert Pitts, had skin transplanted from his chest to his fingertips. This got rid of the fingerprints but he was convicted on other evidence, and the doctor who operated on his fingers went to jail too!

5. The Ancient Chinese knew how to identify people from their fingerprints. They used a thumb print in wax as a 'signature' that couldn't be forged.

6. In 1892 the English scientist Sir Francis Galton wrote the first book on fingerprints. They were first used as evidence in the same year in a Brazilian murder case where the fingerprint was made in the victim's blood. Experiments then showed that fingers leave

23

their invisible pattern on hard, smooth surfaces and special powder can be used to make the patterns show up. Police no longer had to hope the criminal would leave a visible print.

7. Millions of people have been convicted on fingerprint evidence since that first case in 1892. In one classic case in 1948 the police in Blackburn, northern England, created a record when they fingerprinted 46,253 men to catch a killer.

8. It is possible to fake fingerprint evidence. In a 1943 case police in the Bahamas made an arrest after claiming they had found a fingerprint at a murder scene. Then the accused man's own private detective proved that the police had 'transplanted' his print from

a drinking glass to the scene of the crime. He was released.

9. The Federal Bureau of Investigation (FBI) of the United States keeps fingerprint records and now holds about 173 million people on its fingerprint files.

10. Fingerprints should be a foolproof way of proving someone is guilty (or innocent) of a crime. Unfortunately, fingerprint experts can make mistakes. Working eight hours a day, studying those tiny marks, needs great concentration. Mistakes have been made and innocent people have ended up in prison. Fingerprints may be foolproof but the people who read them aren't.

Fingerprints can't be copied

easily. Handwriting can. Police use handwriting specialists (like Hanna Sulner) for advice, but don't consider their evidence to be absolute proof. Handwriting experts can often disagree with one another. That's what happened in a famous kidnapping case.

Sometimes detectives put a case together like a jigsaw. When all the pieces are in place they can see the face of the guilty person. But other, more ruthless, detectives see the face first, then go looking for pieces of jigsaw evidence that fit. If they find pieces that don't fit, they ignore them. And if they can't find the right pieces, they make them up. That may be what happened in America's most famous kidnapping case of all time.

USA, 1934

The man had a haunted look, the look of a man who knows he's going to die. And he was right.

'The jury found you guilty, Mr Hauptmann,' I told him, pushing my hat to the back of my head. 'You can't expect me to save you. I'm a private detective, not Marvo the Magician.'

He turned away from the cold steel bars of his cell and looked at me. 'I know that, Mr Elliot,' he said quietly, speaking with a slight German accent. 'I know they will execute me. They have to execute someone. They have to blame someone. All I want is for my friends and my family to know the truth.'

'But the evidence against you was pretty convincing,' I said. Something about the echo of my voice in that concrete cell made my flesh creep like a walk in a graveyard.

'The police did not give the full story in court,' he said. No bitterness. Just a fact. I guess that's why I believed him. I guess also that I was the only person in the whole US of A who believed that Bruno Hauptmann might just be innocent of kidnapping the Lindbergh baby.

I'd read the newspapers, the same as everyone else. The judge sure didn't believe in Hauptmann's innocence. Judge Quinn loved Hauptmann like Scrooge loved Christmas. His summing up was a work of art, the art of saying, 'We all know he's guilty, so let's give him a fair trial—then execute him!'

What Quinn actually said was, 'Charles Lindbergh is one of the heroes of the American people, the first man to fly solo across the Atlantic Ocean.

He deserved a quiet and happy life with his wife and little son. Instead he found misery and heartbreak as the victim of one of the cruellest crimes of the century. Two years ago, on 1 March 1932, he said goodnight to his nineteen-month-old son Charles—or Buster as his loving parents called him. At 9.10 pm the Lindberghs heard a cracking sound from outside of the house—the sound we now know was the cracking of the kidnapper's ladder, the ladder that plays such an important part in this case. At 10 pm young Buster's nurse discovered an open shutter and little Buster gone from the nursery. She also saw a note on the windowsill. When the police opened it they found a ransom demand for $50,000. In the garden they found the ladder that had been used to reach the window. It was a home-made ladder, in three sections. Where the top section joined the second section the ladder had been broken—the noise the Lindberghs heard.'

How Judge Quinn could know that was the noise they heard was beyond me, but no one challenged him. He went on to describe the ransom pick-up. A guy called John Condon offered to act as go-between for the Lindberghs. The kidnapper contacted Condon and sent him a letter—a letter full of spelling mistakes—and told the go-between to put an ad in the local paper when 'the mony is redy'.

Condon met the masked kidnapper twice. After the first meeting the kidnapper sent the go-between Buster's babysuit to prove he had the kid. Then they met again in a graveyard and Condon handed over

$50,000 in cash and gold certificates. It was one of those gold certificates that sank Hauptmann—the police had a note of all their numbers.

When Judge Quinn described the finding of Buster's dead little body he gave a performance that would have won him an Oscar in Hollywood. Finding Buster dead was the low point of the case for the police. Then, after two years of useless detective work, came the high point. Hauptmann handed over one of the $10 gold certificates for some petrol, the garage attendant made a note of the car number and the car was traced to Hauptmann.

I could see the judge's eyes glowing as he built up the case against Hauptmann. Once the police had a suspect they made all the evidence fit and it fitted like a glove. 'Mr Hauptmann says he was given the money to look after by a friend,' Judge Quinn said. He paused after the word 'says'. He left the jury in no doubt as to what he thought of Hauptmann's story. It's little pauses like that which will hang a man.

Then Judge Quinn reminded the jury about the ladder. A 'wood technologist' called Koehler had traced where the wood for the rungs came from. The newspapers said it was 'the greatest piece of scientific detection of all time'. That wood was sold at a timber yard near to where Hauptmann lived. But the sixteenth rung—oh boy! That really put the final nail in the German's coffin. The police searched Hauptmann's attic and found that a floorboard had been ripped up and sawn. The wood matched the wood of rung 16. Four nail holes in the rung exactly fitted the nail holes of the missing floorboard! Brilliant detective work.

They didn't need any more evidence against Hauptmann, but Judge Quinn threw it in just to pour a few buckets of water over the drowning man. In the cell I tried that evidence on Hauptmann for size.

'You have a criminal record back in Germany,' I told him. 'That's why you ran away and came to America illegally.'

'I was a burglar, not a kidnapper. I have committed no crimes in America.'

'So where did the money come from? They found the Lindbergh kidnap money—or $14,000 of it—in your attic.'

'Whose side are you on?' he said sharply. That made the guard look up and take a step towards him. 'Sorry!' he said quickly.

'I'm on your side, Mr Hauptmann, but I need your side of the story. All I've heard so far is the case for the prosecution.'

'Sure. Sorry,' he muttered and sat down. 'I made a good living as a carpenter. You could check my bank accounts—the police didn't bring them up in court. I was doing fine before the Lindbergh kidnap. I didn't need the money. Why would I want to risk my neck with a crime?'

'Answer my question,' I said.

He sighed. 'A friend called Fisch owed me 7,500 dollars when he went back to Germany. He left me a cardboard box to look after. It got damp in the attic, so I opened it to dry out whatever was in it. That's when I found the money.'

'And helped yourself.'

He spread his hard hands wide. 'It was the money he owed me!'

'And it was also the Lindbergh kidnap money,' I told him.

Hauptmann nodded. 'The money was for sale in the Bronx area where we lived. For four dollars you could buy a ten-dollar gold bond—*if* you were willing to take the risk of getting caught spending it. Fisch must have bought those bonds, then left them with me until the case went out of the news.'

'Nice friends you've got. Where's this Fisch now?'

The man looked down at the table. 'I don't know. Somewhere in Germany.'

'Have you tried to find him?'

'How could I when I'm locked up in here?'

'OK. So did the police try to find him?'

Hauptmann looked up angrily. 'Why *would* they try? They had me. All they were interested in was nailing me.'

'And talking about nails, Mr Hauptmann, how do you explain the ladder?' I said, pushing him hard now he was getting angry. Angry men tell the truth.

'What about the ladder?' he asked.

'Made with wood from your local wood yard,' I said.

'Made with wood that my local wood yard sold . . . along with thirty other wood yards in the state! Yes, the wood could have come from the Bronx, but the kidnapper could have got it from any one of the other thirty yards!'

'The police never said that in court,' I said. 'But then that floorboard from your attic was the clincher.'

He looked me in the face for the first time. His eyes were shadowed with rings as blue as wood smoke. 'Mr Elliot,' he said quietly, 'why would I use a piece of wood from my attic? Why would I rip up a floorboard when I could have simply bought another piece of wood?'

'So who made that rung 16?' I asked.

'Did you know that my wife lived in

the house while the police searched it for clues? But she was so disturbed she moved out. It was *after* she moved out that they say they found that floorboard.'

'You're saying the police ripped up the floorboard and made that rung? The police framed you?' I asked. 'Can you prove that?'

'No. And I can't disprove it either,' he said. 'But I will tell you one thing: that ladder was very badly made. Look at how it cracked when the kidnapper climbed down it.'

'So?'

'So, you are forgetting I am a trained carpenter. I could not make a bad ladder if I tried.' He had a point— another one of those points the jury ignored.

'There was a phone number scribbled on a wall in a cupboard,' I reminded him. 'It was the phone number of Condon, the go-between.'

He spread those hands wide and helpless again. 'Why would I write that number in a cupboard? I have never had a phone in the house! What use is it written there? I don't know who wrote it. All I do know is it wasn't me.'

'OK, Mr Hauptmann, let's look at the ransom notes. The writer couldn't spell. When the police asked you to write the messages you made the same spelling mistakes,' I told him.

'Oh, no, Mr Elliot. The police did not ask me to *write* the messages, they asked me to *copy* them. Complete with the spelling mistakes.'

'They never said that in court either,' I said, shaking my head.

'Like they never said that Condon heard voices in the background when he phoned the kidnapper. Those voices were speaking in Italian,' Hauptmann said.

'Italian? As in Mafia?' I said. 'You think this was a Mafia kidnapping?'

The man shook his head slowly. 'I don't know. All I know is that I didn't do it.'

'The rest of the world seems to disagree, Mr Hauptmann,' I said.

'So you won't help me?'

I thought about it for a while. 'The state governor tried to sack the man who was your prosecutor. The press say the governor is backing an appeal. I'll talk to him and see what he has to say.'

I stood up. Hauptmann stretched out a hand. A large hand, a rough hand. The hand of a carpenter for sure. The hand of a killer? Who knows?

*　　*　　*

'Hauptmann will die,' Governor Hoffman told me. 'The American people were horrified by the death of little Buster. They can't believe an American would do such a thing to the son of their hero.'

'But a German . . .' I said, following his line of thought. 'They'd rather believe a foreigner could do it?'

He nodded. 'Hauptmann will die because the people want someone to blame. I agree with you, all the evidence is very, very suspect. I wouldn't be surprised if the police did manufacture some of it, just as you say. After all, the whole world has told our police they're the greatest detectives in the world to crack this case. They like that. They're not going to admit they're a bunch of crooks, are they? No, Mr Elliot, you should know—a detective's job is to come up with answers. And sometimes detectives come up with answers that people want, not the answers that are the truth. I've done my best to get Hauptmann a fair hearing, and you've done your best, Mr Elliot. But sometimes that's not good enough.'

'So who really killed Buster Lindbergh?' I asked him.

'We don't know,' he said quietly. 'And I have a feeling we never will.'

The Lindbergh kidnapping —FACT FILE

1. Bruno Hauptmann was unlucky. The law was out to make sure he paid for the kidnapping, even if he didn't do it. The child was snatched from the Lindberghs' home in the state of New Jersey. In New Jersey a kidnapper could only be executed if the victim died *while a robbery was being committed*. No one knew when Buster died, so Hauptmann should not have been executed. The prosecutor told the jury Buster had *probably* died in the nursery or when the ladder snapped. They believed him.

2. After the Lindbergh kidnapping the laws were changed to make punishment easier. Anyone committing a kidnap could be executed if the victim suffered any harm at all. Even sending a ransom note could cost twenty years in jail, a $5,000 fine or both.

3. Modern detection has shed new light on the case:

- Hauptmann was telling the truth when he said the money box had been damaged by damp.
- In the 1990s, handwriting experts looked again at Hauptmann's writing and the writing on the kidnap notes. They disagreed with the 1934 expert and said the kidnap notes were almost certainly *not* written by Hauptmann.
- Fisch *did* owe Hauptmann over $7,000 and *was*

42

involved in a lot of illegal deals. Fisch could well have 'bought' the Lindbergh kidnap money that Hauptmann was storing in his attic, but he died in Germany in the year of Hauptmann's trial and so could not be found to back up the accused man's story.

- The wood technologist, Koehler, said that his method of looking at saw marks, wood grain, tree rings, knot holes and nail holes was as sure a proof as fingerprinting. In fact it isn't. This 'greatest feat of scientific detection of all time' is no more accurate than handwriting tests.

4. The governor of the prison, Harold Hoffmann, interviewed Hauptmann several times in his cell and did not believe that the accused man was

guilty. He tried to help the German to prove his case. Hauptmann offered to take truth drugs and lie-detector tests to prove his innocence, but the police refused. Hauptmann was executed in 1935.

5. There is a strange theory that little Buster never died at all. A baby's skeleton was found near an orphanage. It could not be identified, though Buster's nurse said she recognized the rotting shirt in which the baby was wrapped. Was the body in fact one of the orphans? And was Buster actually kidnapped by the Mafia as some people suspected? A baby of the right age was handed by gangsters to a family to raise as their own son. (With the huge hunt that went on for the baby, the kidnappers may have decided

44

it was too risky to try to 'cash in' on him, and they didn't want to kill him.) Before the mother died she told the boy that she believed he was Charles Lindbergh's son. The boy grew up to be Harold Olson. Photographs show that Buster Lindbergh had a scar on his chin and Harold Olson had a scar in exactly the same place.

THE CASE OF THE POISONED PIGS

Think of detectives and you usually think of the police. But some of the greatest puzzles have been solved by the people who help the police—the scientists.

Victoria State, Australia, February 1940

'Somebody poisoned my pig!' the woman said, and she hit the top of the police station counter with a large fist. It was a strong fist. Everything about the middle-aged woman was strong—including her smell, Sergeant Sharp thought. He couldn't help wrinkling his nose a little as he pulled out a pencil.

'Name, madam?' he asked, opening the report book to note the details.

'Blenkinsop. Alicia Blenkinsop,' the woman said, pulling her overall round her large chest. Her face was as brown and tough as boot leather. Her eyes were pale blue marbles, sunken and small in folds of fat.

'Address, Mrs Blenkinsop?'

'Yarra Glen Model Pig Farm.'

'And what seems to be the problem?' the policeman asked as he leaned back

48

out of the way of the woman's pig-swill scent. It was hot in this small station and the summer air was suffocating enough. The young sergeant ran a finger under his collar and wished he could get a job in one of those patrol cars. That was the life!

Instead he was stuck in here with this woman talking to him. No, not talking—shouting. 'I just *told* you, somebody poisoned my pig! Not an ordinary pig, a valuable *prize* pig!' Every time she said the letter 'p' she sprayed Doug Sharp's face with spittle. He leaned back further. 'A *pedigree* pig!' she finished.

'You sure it's poison? Couldn't have been natural causes?' he asked. It wasn't often he had the chance to play detective and he was going to make the most of it.

'Sergeant,' she said, 'I've worked with pigs for twenty years . . .'

And never had a bath in all that time, he thought.

'Twenty years. And I know a poisoned pig when I see one! It was lying on its back, legs in the air and

49

belly swollen like it had swallowed a football. *Poison*!' she said, spraying the policeman again. 'Poison by persons unknown.' She leaned forward and finished dramatically, 'Murder!'

Sergeant Sharp used his pencil to scratch his neck. 'I'm not sure the death of a pig—'

'A *prize* pig!' she reminded him.

'A *prize* pig . . . I'm not sure that is classed as homicide. Maybe you should talk to the animal cruelty people. Or a vet.'

'Maybe it's not homicide. Maybe it's pigicide, whatever. It was a *crime*.'

'Have you any idea when the crime was committed?' the policeman asked.

'Last night,' Mrs Blenkinsop said quickly. 'I was lying in bed, windows open 'cos of the heat, and I heard a car coming down the track. Heard it stop near the pigsties then move off again, fast.'

'What time?'

'Didn't notice. Didn't think it was important at the time,' the woman shrugged.

'I see,' Doug Sharp nodded. If he

50

was going to play detective then he knew he had to work out something called 'motive'. 'Any idea why someone might want to kill your pig?'

Mrs Blenkinsop's little blue eyes popped. She leaned forward and brought her face close to the young sergeant. 'Nazis!' she hissed. 'Spies!'

The policeman's mouth dropped open. 'Nazi spies killed your pig, Mrs Blenkinsop? Why would they want to do that?'

'We're at war, aren't we?' she said as if that was enough answer.

'Yes, but—'

'And every pound of pig meat is part of the war effort, isn't it? 'Specially prize breeding pigs. It's called sabotage,' she said. 'So you get yourself out to Yarra Glen and investigate. OK?'

'Er . . . yes, Mrs Blenkinsop,' Doug Sharp said.

*   *   *

After the woman left, the policeman opened all the doors and windows to

51

freshen the air, then put his head around the door of Detective Inspector Drysdale's office. 'Murder case, sir,' he said.

'Murder?' the detective said, raising a lazy eyebrow.

'Seems we have some Nazi spies trying to ruin the country by poisoning our pigs.'

Drysdale's interested eyebrow dropped. 'Ah, yeah. Lot of them about.'

'Seriously, sir. Who do I see about a pig-poisoning case?'

The inspector pulled a blue-backed book from a drawer and ran a finger down the list of names and phone numbers. 'Here's the guy: Charles Taylor, Victoria's Public Analyst. Knows more about poisons than anyone in Australia.'

'Yes, sir,' the sergeant said, taking the slip of paper with the telephone number.

'Oh, but Sharp . . .'

'Yes, sir?'

'If he offers you a cup of tea, don't drink it.'

'Very funny, sir.'

'And Sharp!'

'Yes, sir?'

'Are you responsible for that disgusting smell?'

The sergeant turned red to the roots of his sun-bleached hair. 'Sorry, sir,' he muttered as he backed out of the door.

*   *   *

It took Sergeant Sharp a long time to persuade Charles Taylor to accompany him to Yarra Glen. 'I'm extremely busy,' the man insisted.

'But they're pedigree pigs, Mr Taylor. Important to the war effort.'

There was a long silence on the other end of the phone, then a sigh. 'Very well. I'll meet you at Yarra Glen tomorrow morning.'

The next morning it seemed that word had got around the small farms in the area. Every farmer for ten miles around had turned up with his family to see the famous Mr Charles Taylor at work. Mrs Blenkinsop stood proudly in her back yard, telling her visitors about the spies who came in the night. The sun burned on the baked soil and made the smell of the dead pig worse than ever.

Sergeant Sharp arrived first. Mrs Blenkinsop marched up to him. 'Another one last night!' she said. 'I'll be ruined at this rate.'

'Another one?' Doug asked, then wished he hadn't. He groped for a handkerchief to mop the spray he knew was coming.

'Porker!' she said. 'Pedigree prize porker. Want to see it?'

Doug Sharp didn't want to see it and was glad when the sound of a car engine announced the arrival of Charles Taylor.

The group in the back yard fell silent and waited for the words of wisdom from the great man.

He stood in the yard and looked around slowly, a wide-brimmed hat shading his sharp eyes. After two minutes he stepped across to the sergeant and shook hands. 'Morning,' he said shortly.

'Good morning, sir. Would you like to see the pig? Another one died this morning.'

'Hmm,' Taylor said and gave the dead pig a quick glance. 'Let's look at the layout first, shall we?'

'The layout?' Doug Sharp asked.

'That's right. Ever want to be a detective, Sergeant?' the scientist asked.

'Why, yes, sir!' the young man replied eagerly.

'Then start by looking at the scene of the crime,' Charles Taylor advised. In a heat that made the distant mountains shimmer the poisons expert was as cool as the Tasman Sea. 'Why do you think the pig pens were built just there?' he asked.

'Would it be the trees?' the young sergeant guessed.

Taylor nodded. 'Good. These ironbark gums are the tallest trees for quite a distance. The pens were built in the shade of the trees. Let's see if there's anything in the soil that could harm the animals, shall we?'

As the silent crowd looked on, the scientist knelt and scooped up a handful of soil from inside the pen.

Even the pigs stopped eating to watch as he rubbed it between his fingers and sniffed carefully. 'Healthy enough soil, pure water. You can tell by the healthy trees that are growing here,' he said. Suddenly something caught his eye: a bright ball of rainbow fluff. He swooped to pick it up and slipped it into his pocket before the watchers could make out quite what it was.

He raised a lazy hand and pointed to a small mound a hundred metres or so from the pig pens. 'Now, those trees over there don't look so healthy, do they?'

'No, sir,' Sergeant Sharp agreed, looking at the scrawny, dwarfed plants covering the low hill.

'Let's have a look at that hill, shall we?' Taylor said and set off without waiting for an answer. Rosella parrots rose in a screeching, brilliant cloud as the men approached the mound and Charles Taylor crouched to feel the soil. 'Sandy soil. And look at this,' he said, holding out a handful. 'See those crystals? That's the sort of gritty stuff those parrots need in their diet. Helps them to make the eggshells in their bodies. I think a sample of that will be interesting,' and he scooped a small amount into his pocket.

Mrs Blenkinsop was scowling by the time he returned to her back yard. 'Ain't you going to look at my poor pig?' she asked.

'I don't think so,' the scientist said.

'It's *dead*!' the woman wailed. 'Ain't you going to examine the *corpse?*'

'No. I can see that it's dead, and I will try to ascertain the cause,' Taylor promised.

'By looking at a hill a hundred yards away?' she screeched in disbelief. 'The pigs don't eat over there. They've been poisoned in their pens by Nazi spies!'

Charles Taylor gave the woman a polite smile, raised his hat and said, 'Good day, Mrs Blenkinsop. Sergeant Sharp here will be in touch.'

A group of farmers were left shaking their heads as the scientist climbed into his car and drove the forty kilometres back to Melbourne.

*　　*　　*

As the day cooled into evening Doug Sharp received a message from Charles Taylor—an invitation to visit him at his laboratory in the city. The policeman arrived at eight and the scientist showed him into the room. The chemical smells were almost as disgusting as Mrs Blenkinsop's dead pig.

'Well, Sergeant, have you solved the case yet?' Taylor asked, and his eyes sparkled behind the wire-rimmed glasses.

'No . . . have you?' the policeman asked.

'If I give you all of the evidence that I have, perhaps you can crack the curious case of the poisoned pigs. Sounds like something Sherlock Holmes would be interested in,' the older man smiled. He took the policeman across to a work bench and showed him two small samples of dark crystals. 'These crystals are from the soil we found by the stunted trees,' he explained. 'Put some into this liquid for me, will you?'

Sergeant Sharp took a small spoon and carefully scooped some crystals into a test-tube full of a clear liquid. The liquid turned bright orange. 'Now, Sergeant, that only happens if the crystals are of a substance called stibnite. It's usually buried deep underground, but it can be brought to the surface during mining work. That small mound was waste from a long-gone mine. Now try this other sample of crystals.'

The policeman took a second sample and tipped the crystals into a fresh tube of liquid. The liquid turned bright orange again. 'More stibnite?' he asked.

'Exactly. But this second sample was from the object I picked up inside the pig pen.'

'Yeah!' Doug Sharp said. 'What exactly was that?'

The professor uncovered a small bundle of feathers on the end of the bench. 'A Rosella parrot. Those crystals came from its stomach. Now, you have all the facts . . . solve the case.'

The policeman sat on a laboratory stool and stared at the two orange test-tubes. 'Is stibnite poisonous?' he asked suddenly.

'Very,' the scientist nodded.

Doug Sharp took a deep breath and began to untangle the problem. 'The old mine workings left the ground poisoned, so trees wouldn't grow properly. That's why Mrs Blenkinsop chose the ironbark gum trees for her pig shade. And that's why the parrots chose the same trees to nest in.'

'Good,' Charles Taylor said. 'We'll make a detective out of you yet.'

'The parrots flew across to the poisoned ground and got a gut full of stibnite. They flew back to the ironbark gum trees to nest, died of stibnite poisoning and fell into the pig pens.

60

The pigs ate the bodies of the parrots and died too!'

'Brilliant!' the scientist laughed and clapped his hands softly. 'You should be pleased with yourself, Sergeant!'

'Yeah. I just wish they'd been kookaburras, a lyre bird or even a frogmouth—anything but a pigeon or a parrot.'

'Why is that, Sergeant?'

'Oh, Mrs Blenkinsop has a little trouble with the letter "p",' he said.

*　　*　　*

'Parrots? Perishing parrots poisoned my prize pedigree pigs!' Mrs Blenkinsop exploded.

Sergeant Doug Sharp wiped his face with a handkerchief. 'I was afraid you'd say that,' he muttered.

*　　*　　*

The Yarra Glen poisoning case was taken very seriously at the time. The Prime Minister of Victoria State took a personal interest and was as worried as

61

the pig farmer that the pigs might be the victims of Nazi saboteurs. He used his power to order Charles Anthony Taylor of Melbourne University to assist the police. Taylor was known as 'The Cat' because of his cunning brain and because of his initials, and he solved many cases that puzzled the police.

Detectives and poison—
FACT FILE

1.   Experts in the study of poisons are known as toxicologists. The toxicologist's job is to separate a poison from the victim's stomach or blood and to say what type of poison it is. Modern toxicology is so sophisticated that even tiny amounts of poison can be detected. The detective's job is to find where the poisoner got the poison from and to prove that he gave it to the victim. The chance of a poisoner succeeding today is not as great as it used to be.

2. Detectives are trained to examine the scene of a sudden death very carefully for poison. Medicines found near the victim are labelled and sent for testing by toxicologists. Cups, bottles or glasses are drained and their contents tested, and detectives note any dangerous substances in an unusual place—car anti-freeze in the kitchen or weed-killer in the bedroom, say. They may also look at tea, coffee or sugar jars and smell them for anything unusual. They are, of course, told never to try tasting them!

3. Poisoning has always been considered a particularly vicious way to kill somebody. The poisoner usually has to be in close contact with the victim if they are to give them the poison. That often

64

means it is a wife, husband, relative or close friend. For this reason the chances of detecting a poisoner are usually greater. A famous case in Tudor England concerned Alice Arden, who was convicted of poisoning her husband in 1551. Killing someone so close to you was believed to be nastier than, say, a robber killing an unknown victim, so the punishment was much nastier than usual. Alice Arden was sentenced to be burned alive.

4. Other unpopular poisoners had their executions recorded by poets. These people wrote verses about the killer which usually damned him, gloated over his death and said it was a warning to others. They were printed and sold for a penny. A typical example was *The Execution of Alice Holt:*

A dreadful case of poison, such as we seldom hear,
Committed was at Stockport, in the county of Cheshire,
Where a mother named Mary Bailey, they did so cruelly slaughter,
By poison administered all in her beer, by her own daughter.
The daughter insured the life of her mother, for £26 at her death,
Then she and the man she lived with determined to take away her breath.
She made a plan to murder her, as we now see so clear,
To put a quantity of arsenic into her poor mother's beer.

But there's no doubt the base wretch did her poor mother slay,
For which on Chester scaffold her life did forfeit pay.
So all young women a warning take, by this poor wretch you

see,
A-hanging for her mother's sake on Chester's fatal tree.

The poisoning was a nasty crime . . . and that sort of verse was a bit of a crime against the art of poetry!

5. The poison arsenic was invented by an Arab chemist. It was used in killing flies and in making beauty treatments, so it was widely available. A certain amount of arsenic is naturally present in the human body and in certain foods we eat and is harmless in small quantities. Some people used to eat small quantities of the poison as a tonic to make them feel fit! But arsenic is poisonous in doses of more than 65mg. Many famous poisoners used arsenic because it had little taste and could be mixed with food. Then, when the

victim began to die, their doctor would often believe they had a natural stomach illness, often called 'gastric fever'.

The disadvantage of using arsenic as a poison was that victims would have traces of arsenic in their hair, nails or bones long after they had been buried. Some poisoners were detected in this way years after they thought they had 'got away with murder'. That's what happened in a famous English case.

Poisoning used to be a popular way of getting rid of an unwanted person because the killer could be many miles away by the time his victim died. In many cases doctors would conclude that the victim had died of natural causes. Some poisoners saw their victims buried and would have got away with their crime if they hadn't become over-confident and tried to do it again.

Hay-on-Wye, England, 1922

'Twenty packets of arsenic, please,' the small man ordered. He looked as if he was used to giving orders, a military man with a back as stiff and straight as his walking cane and a moustache that bristled like the back of an angry cat.

'You'll have to sign the poisons book, Major,' Edward Mann the chemist said as he reached for the arsenic jar and began to measure out the white powder.

'Of course, of course!' Major Armstrong barked.

The chemist squinted carefully at the

scales as he let the powder drop into the brass pan. 'More than 65 milligrams can kill a man,' he warned. He tipped the measured powder on to a small square of paper and folded it carefully, then began to measure out the second portion. 'And you don't have to swallow it,' he went on. 'You can poison yourself by breathing in the dust.'

'Don't worry,' Major Armstrong said. 'I place it in a squirt gun with a pointed nozzle. I then insert the nozzle into the ground at the root of the dandelion and squirt. Kills the dandelion but not the grass around it. I hate dandelions. Hate them, hate them!' he said, and his blue eyes glittered behind his gold-rimmed glasses.

Edward Mann folded the second packet and carried on working while he talked slowly to his customer. 'Sickness and diarrhoea,' he said, 'they're the first signs of arsenic poisoning. So if you feel the first sign of sickness, see your doctor.'

'Fit as a flea! Fit as a flea!' The

major gave a barking laugh but his eyes never left the packets of deadly powder as they piled up on the chemist's workbench.

'There you are!' Edward Mann said finally. 'Twenty packets of arsenic.'

The small major gave a satisfied twist to the end of his moustache. 'Twenty dead dandelions,' he said grimly. He signed the poison register and picked up the brown-paper bag, then, with a 'Good day to you, Mr Mann,' he raised his hat politely and marched out of the chemist's shop.

*   *   *

'Funny chap, that Major Armstrong,' Edward Mann said that evening as he ate supper with his daughter Eunice and her husband Arthur Martin. 'His office is across the road from yours, isn't it, Arthur?'

Arthur had a long, sad face like an overworked horse. 'It is. And I wish it wasn't. We're the only two solicitors in town and there's more than enough work for both of us, yet he seems to see

72

me as some kind of rival.' The young man leaned forward and said quietly, 'He watches me.'

'You never said, Arthur!' Eunice put in. She had a plump and worried face. Her eyes grew wide with wonder.

'Sometimes I look up from my desk and I see him standing at the window of his office, staring.'

'Staring?'

'Staring straight at me,' Arthur said.

'Ooh, Arthur! And he has those creepy pale blue eyes, doesn't he?'

'He does,' Arthur nodded his cart-horse head. 'But why do you say he's a funny chap, Dad?' the young solicitor asked his father-in-law.

'Because he has an obsession about dandelions. Says he hates them,' Edward Mann explained.

'Ooh! Yes, he would,' Eunice nodded and her plump chin trembled a little. 'He lives in that huge house at the end of the town. "Mayfield" it's called. Bea-oooo-tiful lawns. Seems to be a hobby with him.'

'Hobby!' her father snorted. 'More like an obsession. Still, he must be

73

doing well from that solicitor business,' he went on, nudging Arthur in the ribs with an elbow. 'You'll be buying a big house for Eunice when you're that rich, I expect.'

Arthur shook his long, worried head. 'I don't make that much money,' he said, 'and the major seems to have even fewer clients than I do.'

'So where does he get his money from?' Edward Mann asked.

'His wife—his *late* wife, I should say,' Eunice explained. 'Poor woman died last February. Changed her will just before she died. Left all her money to the major.' She leaned forward over the tea table and said quietly, 'He *earned* her money, by all accounts.'

'How do you mean, my dear?' her husband asked.

'She gave him a terrible life. *Terrible.* She wouldn't let him smoke or drink in the house. And when he was up at the tennis club she'd show him up something rotten. More than once she came and dragged him off the tennis court if he was two minutes late for dinner!'

Edward Mann blinked. In that blink he saw the major's pale blue eyes glittering behind gold-rimmed glasses. He saw arsenic powder . . . and he saw a dead woman. He blinked again and tried to forget the disturbing picture. Luckily for Eunice and Arthur, he didn't forget it entirely.

*   *   *

Two weeks later Arthur fell ill.

Eunice chewed the corner of a handkerchief as she tried to tell her father why he wouldn't be joining them for supper that night. 'The doctor gave him bicarbonate of soda but it hasn't settled him. He's being terribly sick.'

Edward Mann frowned. 'What has he been eating?' he asked.

'Nothing that I haven't eaten too,' she sniffed. Suddenly her eyes began to glisten with tears. 'You're not saying my cooking has made him ill?' she said.

He wrapped an arm around her shoulder. 'No, no. But he must sometimes eat outside the house. Let's ask him, shall we?'

She sniffed and nodded. The chemist and his daughter climbed the dark stairway to the small bedroom. Arthur's bed was a tangled mess and the young solicitor was thrashing about wildly, groaning and clutching his stomach. The chemist looked into the sick bowl by the bedside. 'Here, Father, I'll take that away,' Eunice said, reaching for the bowl.

'Scones!' her husband cried suddenly.

'Scones? You want me to cook you some scones?' Eunice asked.

'Scones. Went to tea . . . with Major Armstrong . . . discussing a case . . . gave me a scone . . . strange!' Arthur gasped.

'That was nice of him,' Eunice said, adding quietly to her father, 'He's been having these strange hallucinations.'

Edward Mann leaned forward. 'What was strange about the scone, Arthur?' he asked carefully.

'He handed me the scone . . . he didn't pass the plate . . . "Excuse my fingers," he said . . . handed me the scone.'

'I see,' the chemist breathed. 'He wanted you to have that particular scone, did he?'

Arthur made a huge effort, turned his head and looked into the eyes of his father-in-law. 'Poison!' he managed to say.

Eunice gave a small gasp. 'Should we send him to the hospital?' she asked.

'No. We have everything we need in the shop downstairs,' he said briskly. 'We'll test for the poison and give him the right cure much quicker than any hospital could. Fetch Arthur's bowl,' he ordered. 'Just as well you didn't throw it away.'

The chemist bounded down the stairs and Eunice scrambled after him. He unlocked the door into his workshop and began assembling the apparatus he would need. He spoke quickly. 'Eunice, you used to help me in the shop when you were younger. I'll need your help now.'

'Yes, Father. What do you want me to do?'

'Take some of the contents of the bowl and pour it through a funnel into

77

a test-tube,' he ordered while he selected a bottle of pale golden liquid and lit a gas burner under a glass jar.

'But you can't test for every poison,' Eunice said as she began the unpleasant task of filling the test-tube.

'You're right. I'll test for just one. If that is negative we'll send for the ambulance,' he said. 'Now, add half of the contents of the test-tube to the liquid in this jar.'

'What is it?'

'Hydrochloric acid,' he said. 'Hurry, girl!'

He didn't usually speak to her so sharply. She tipped some of her test-tube contents into the boiling acid and stepped back. Her father stirred it with a glass rod, then took it away from the heat. Then he took a thin strip of copper from his cupboard and dipped it into the mixture in the jar. He removed it ten seconds later. It was covered with a dull, grey coating.

'This is called Reinsch's test,' he explained. 'And that grey coating proves that your husband has swallowed arsenic.'

*　　*　　*

The police inspector sat in the armchair and looked at the three worried people. 'Yes, Mr Mann, our tests confirm that your son-in-law has swallowed arsenic. Indeed he is lucky to be alive. Your prompt action probably saved him.'

Eunice squeezed her father's hand and smiled faintly at her husband.

'You'll arrest Major Armstrong, then?' she said.

Inspector Harris shook his head. 'Madam, we cannot go around arresting respectable citizens like the major without evidence.'

The chemist rose to his feet, agitated. 'He gave my son-in-law the poisoned scone . . .'

'You say he gave the young gentleman a scone, but can you prove that? Then, can you prove that scone was poisoned?'

'No, but . . . I can prove that he bought arsenic from my shop.'

'And how many other people have

79

bought arsenic from how many other shops in this country?' the policeman asked. Edward Mann stayed silent. 'You see, sir, we have no link between the arsenic the major bought and the arsenic found in your son-in-law's stomach. And then the court would expect you to establish a motive. Why would the major want to kill Mr Martin?'

'We are in dispute over a legal matter between one of his clients and one of mine,' Arthur Martin said quickly.

'Hardly a reason to kill you. And you did stay on friendly terms. Why, he even invited you to tea!' the policeman pointed out.

'And what about the chocolates?' Eunice put in.

'Ah, the chocolates,' Inspector Harris said. 'You received a gift of chocolates in the post. The sender did not enclose his or her name. You don't eat chocolates so you placed them on the dinner table for guests. Your guests were very sick afterwards. Well, we shall take the remaining chocolates away for examination, but even if they do contain arsenic you cannot prove they were sent by the major.'

The chemist spoke up. 'What you need is a clear link with Major Armstrong. You need a strong reason for the major to poison someone, and a body—a dead body—full of arsenic,' he concluded.

'Precisely, sir.'

'Then I think I can tell you exactly where you'll find such a body,' the chemist said.

* * *

Arthur Martin hung up the telephone earpiece with difficulty. His hand was trembling. He was paler than he had been when he was suffering from poisoning.

'It was Major Armstrong, wasn't it?' Eunice asked.

'He wants me to come to tea,' her husband said.

'You didn't accept?' she gasped.

'He said we have a case to discuss. Would I come to tea at his house.

That's the third time this week he's invited me.' The young solicitor's haunted eyes met his wife's. 'I'm running out of excuses to refuse, Eunice! And he's still watching me. Everywhere I go he is watching me. I imagine arsenic in everything I eat. My nerves can't stand the strain much longer!' he moaned.

Edward Mann stepped through the doorway from his shop and walked across to where his son-in-law sat trembling by the telephone. 'Not much longer now, Arthur. The police will dig up the body tonight. I will be there as a witness.'

'When will they know the results?' Eunice asked.

'I think you will find they know as soon as they open the coffin,' the chemist assured her.

*   *   *

Inspector Harris introduced the men quickly. 'Mr Mann, this is Sir Bernard Spillsbury, England's leading expert on post-mortem examinations.'

The chemist shook his hand but said nothing. He simply turned to watch the four policemen in shirt-sleeves as they took turns to dig through the damp soil of the grave.

Anyone walking past the churchyard would have been horrified at the sight of the men gathered round the grave like bodysnatchers of old. Only three lanterns lit their work. They had chosen to dig at night rather than let the whole town know their business.

Finally the coffin was hauled to the surface. Inspector Harris brushed loose soil from the name plate. 'Mrs Jane Armstrong,' he read. 'Yes, this is the major's wife. Let's have a quick look before we take her to your laboratory,

Sir Bernard.'

The policeman began to unscrew the coffin lid very carefully. Finally the men stepped forward with a lantern and looked in. 'Died last February?' Sir Bernard asked.

'That's correct,' the inspector said.

'Then her body is beautifully preserved. Too well preserved. Arsenic poisoning does that to a body.' The expert looked at the chemist and said, 'You will be relieved to hear, sir, that Major Armstrong has a case to answer. A case of murder.'

FACT FILE

Serial poisoners—FACT FILE

1. Mrs Armstrong's body was indeed full of arsenic poison. The major was arrested and the full horror of his crimes became clear. He had altered his wife's will so that he gained her considerable fortune when she died. His business was doing badly at the time and he needed the money. The local doctor had concluded that Mrs Armstrong had died naturally and she was buried. The major had got away with murder . . . so he tried again. He argued with a businessman called Davies, invited him to tea and

poisoned him. Davies died and his doctor found the cause of death to be appendicitis. Major Armstrong had got away with murder again! When he wanted rid of Arthur Martin, the only competition in Hay town, he sent poisoned chocolates. They didn't work, but the poisoned scone very nearly did. Only the experienced eye of young Martin's father-in-law, the chemist, recognized the effects of arsenic. Major Armstrong was executed and Martin was saved. He and the dandelions lived to fight another year!

2. The police do sometimes catch poisoners without the help of local chemists. Samuel Doss died in Tulsa, Oklahoma, in 1954 after eating a plate of prunes. On examining his body the police doctor found enough poison

in his stomach to kill ten men. Mrs Doss was shocked. 'How on earth did that happen?' she wanted to know. The police suggested that perhaps she had slipped the poison into the prunes. 'My conscience is clear,' she said. Then they did a little digging into her past and found that *four* husbands before Doss had all died with stomach pains, as well as her mother, two sisters and three other children! She was another poisoner who just kept on poisoning until she was caught. Many famous poisoners seem to keep on poisoning people even when they have no need to.

3. A doctor called Palmer murdered a friend called Cook in 1855. The examination of Cook's body was a joke! Palmer, being a friend of the dead man as

well as a doctor, was allowed to be present at the examination. Cook's stomach was full of strychnine poison but as it was lifted from the body, Palmer gave the surgeon a push and the contents spilled on to the floor! Cook was the last of a long line of Palmer's victims; later investigation showed he was the fourteenth! The doctor might have escaped again but at Cook's examination he tried to bribe the magistrate and the police at last became suspicious. He was executed.

4. Another deadly doctor was Neill Cream. He was practising in America when he poisoned one of his patients. Instead of being executed he was sentenced to prison and released in less than ten years. He decided to continue his criminal habit in

England. In 1892 he began poisoning women. After four deaths he seemed somehow disappointed that the police were nowhere near catching him. He went to New Scotland Yard and said he was being followed by villains, and asked for a detective to accompany him. The more friendly the detective became, the more Cream gave himself away. But the final proof came from a young woman who did *not* die from Cream's poison tablets—she'd thrown them in the Thames and lived. Her evidence led to his execution.

5. Clever poisoners could beat the Reinsch test for arsenic. A doctor called Smethurst married an older woman in 1859 and began to poison her with arsenic so that he could inherit her

money. The woman's own doctor, Doctor Bird, suspected arsenic poisoning and the police arrested Doctor Smethurst for attempted murder. There was no proof at that stage so the magistrate released Smethurst, giving him the chance to finish the job of poisoning his wife! He cleverly disguised the arsenic by adding chlorate of potash to it and this defeated the Reinsch test. There was a lot of arsenic in the poor woman's body but the potash trick confused the case and Smethurst was set free.

A detective's work is not always as exciting and interesting as it is made to appear in books, films or television. One of a detective's main areas of work is 'surveillance'—watching a criminal or a place where you believe a crime might be committed. This is often a long, boring and uncomfortable task. When it succeeds, of course, the effort seems worthwhile.

London, 1924

When I was a young copper I made a big mistake. I was lucky. I learned from my mistake. I never made that mistake again and I became a better policeman as a result. Let me tell you about it.

I'd just been selected to join London's Flying Squad—at least that's what the newspapers called our section. Our correct title was Mobile Patrol Squad, but no one ever called us that.

I was thrilled! The squad was made up of the best detectives in the fastest cars. They didn't just examine crimes and try to catch the criminals, they went out and stopped crime before it happened. They kept a secret watch on known criminals, and even drank with them in local pubs—in disguise, of course.

After spending two years based at an ordinary police station in the East End of London, I was itching for the sort of excitement the Flying Squad seemed to offer: car chases with desperate criminals, arresting dangerous and violent men and being at the scene of big crimes when they happened.

I was disappointed, of course. The Flying Squad got results from hard work, long hours and a lot of boring routine.

I was almost ready to pack it in and go back to my old job when I was given an 'observation' job.

The chief inspector spoke to a dozen of the squad on a Thursday morning in October. 'There are some areas of London that are so rich they attract a thief like jam attracts a wasp. Mayfair is one, St James's another.'

We knew that, of course. Why was he telling us? I shifted in my seat and waited for him to get to the point. 'There is some evidence that many of the burglaries in Mayfair are being carried out by the same man. The same method is used each time, and it's very successful. In the past five weeks we reckon he's got away with £30,000 worth of cash and jewellery.'

£30,000! That was an absolute fortune in 1924, you have to remember. The rest of the detectives sat up too. 'How does he do it?' Bob Fabian asked quickly.

Bob was sharp. He'd joined the squad at the same time as me but he was much brighter. The chief inspector gave a thin smile. 'I wish we knew. Most of the robberies are from hotel bedrooms. When the residents go down to dinner in the evening, our friend comes in through the window and leaves the same way.'

There seemed to be a dozen questions at once.

'He must have a ladder,' one detective chipped in. 'And you can't walk through the London streets with a ladder without being stopped by a

94

policeman on the beat, can you?'

'He seems to go over the roofs and climb *without* a ladder,' the chief inspector said.

'More like a cat,' someone joked. We laughed, but the name stuck. From then on he was nicknamed the Cat Burglar.

'But Mayfair's a wealthy area,' Bob argued. 'Surely a burglar couldn't wander along without being noticed?'

'Maybe he's disguised,' I guessed.

Some of the others shook their heads as if it were a stupid idea and I blushed and wished I hadn't spoken. Bob Fabian came to my rescue. He took me seriously. 'He must be,' he agreed. 'What disguise could he use that would let him walk through Mayfair without being stopped and questioned?'

The chief inspector shrugged. 'If we knew that, then we'd probably catch him.'

'What are we going to do about him?' someone asked.

'We're going to keep a watch on all the big hotels. We'll hide and look out for anything suspicious.'

I groaned softly to myself. I'd joined the Flying Squad looking for excitement. Instead I was going to spend hour after hour, night after night, sitting in the cold and dark looking for an invisible man.

'You will work in pairs,' the chief inspector was saying. 'We'll only cover half as many hotels that way, but at least you'll keep each other awake. And you'll be in a stronger position to make an arrest. If this man's a climber then you can bet he'll be strong as an ox. It might well take two of you to hold him!'

That was a worry. But the good news was that I was paired with Bob Fabian.

*   *   *

We were given the famous Ritz Hotel to watch. We sat among the dustbins in the dark back yard. The sour smell of stale food mixed with the mouth-watering scents from the hotel kitchens.

Bob kept me cheerful but he

couldn't take away the cold and the stiffness. By the time we went home in the morning I was ready to resign. That second night I began to wish that the Cat Burglar would appear. I didn't want someone to be robbed, you understand; I just wanted the excitement of the chase and the thrill of the arrest.

At the same time I was sure we were like cats sitting waiting at an empty mousehole. I was bored. But Bob Fabian was a better detective. He had endless patience. Even while he was chatting his eyes never stopped scanning the curtained windows and the darkened gardens below them. Suddenly he stopped in the middle of a sentence and gripped my arm.

His other hand was pointing towards the back of the houses in Arlington Street. I screwed up my eyes and saw a shadow moving within the shadows. Someone was entering the back gate.

The figure was moving too carefully to be the owner of the house. Bob and I rose to our feet. I forgot about my stiffness and the cold. I forgot about

97

resigning. This was the chase. This was what I'd joined the Flying Squad for.

We followed as quietly and quickly as we could. We entered the garden just in time to see the man climb a high fence and disappear over the far side. When I reached it I realized there was no way I could ever climb it! The man wasn't a cat—he climbed more like a spider!

'We've lost him!' I groaned.

Bob nodded. 'At least we know his disguise,' he said quietly.

'We do?'

'Yes. Didn't you see the glint of a diamond button on the front of a white shirt?' he asked.

'Ah . . . yes,' I lied. I'd been too busy looking at my feet to take proper note of the man's appearance.

'He dresses like a gentleman: black suit, white starched shirt with fancy buttons. No one would ever think of stopping him in Mayfair to ask about a burglary.'

'No,' I agreed.

'Stay in the back street,' Bob ordered. He seemed to know what to do, so I didn't mind him taking charge.

'Where are you going?' I asked quickly. I didn't fancy coming face to face with the man who could climb that fence.

'I'll warn the owners of these houses to check their valuables,' he said as he hurried off down the dim lane.

I stared up at the backs of the houses. Now my tired eyes were sharp as a sparrow-hawk's. The Flying Squad cars had radios and I wished I'd had one there. If the rest of the squad could be brought in to surround the street, then we'd have caught the burglar there and then.

Instead I had to watch, helpless, as the Cat Burglar appeared on a balcony. I waited for him to drop down and hurry through the garden, out of the gate and into my waiting arms. My heart was beating so hard I could feel the blood pounding through my head. My handcuffs jangled in my trembling hands and I almost dropped them.

To my amazement he didn't climb down. Instead he threw something up to the roof, climbed up it and vanished over the rooftops. I'm ashamed to admit it, but I felt relieved I didn't have to tackle him alone.

I was even more ashamed the next morning when I found he'd escaped with over £2,000-worth of jewellery. Of course we were the centre of attention when we got back to headquarters. Bob's information about the Cat Burglar's smart clothes was vital.

'The strange thing is that he was wearing soft rubber soles on his shoes,' Bob said.

'How do you know?' someone asked.

'I checked the balcony for footprints,' my partner explained.

'Yes. That is strange,' the chief inspector nodded.

'But why?' I had to ask. I knew I should have worked it out for myself but remember, I was still young in those days.

Bob smiled. 'This man takes a lot of trouble to wear smart evening clothes. That should include smart leather shoes, otherwise he'd look odd. Smart shoes have leather soles. Yet he has crêpe rubber soles on his shoes to grip

while he's climbing.'

'So we're looking for a man in smart clothes with odd shoes?' I asked stupidly.

'Or we're looking for a pair of smart shoes especially made with rubber soles!' the chief inspector said excitedly.

Bob nodded. He knew that all along. I wish he'd told me instead of letting me make all the wrong guesses. No one noticed my slowness. They were as excited as the chief inspector.

'If we have to question every

shoemaker in London we'll find who owns those shoes!' the chief inspector said. Another long and tiring job! How did I ever imagine the Flying Squad would be exciting?

In fact Bob Fabian had his usual luck. Don't get me wrong, Bob was a brilliant detective, but he had the greatest quality any detective could have. Luck!

We could have searched for weeks. In fact Bob came across the answer in just a day and a half.

*　　*　　*

The shoemaker had a shop in Albermarle Street. We entered and asked the usual question, 'Have you made a pair of smart shoes with crêpe soles?'

We expected the usual answer, that no one ever has crêpe soles on evening shoes. But this time the old man smiled a wrinkled, puzzled smile. 'Now, it's strange you should ask that. A gentleman bought a pair just a month ago.'

I think I stopped breathing for half a minute while Bob Fabian asked softly, 'And do you know the man's address?'

The shoemaker nodded. 'Of course, sir,' and he opened an old cash book. He ran his finger up the list of entries. 'Yes, here it is!'

We hurried from the shop with the address copied carefully on to a piece of paper. 'It was so easy!' I grinned.

Bob didn't smile. 'Nothing's ever that easy,' he said. 'If you were as clever as this thief, would you give your correct name?'

'Why . . . no,' I admitted.

'And you might not even give your right address.'

My heart sank. 'So that name and address is worse than useless? We've just wasted two days?'

'No, no, no!' Bob said. 'The shoemaker described the man, didn't he? His height, his appearance and, most important of all, his American accent.'

'That's not a lot to go on. Where do we start?'

'At this address, of course,' Bob

103

Fabian said briskly. '27 Half Moon Street.'

The woman at 27 Half Moon Street lived alone. She was sixty years old and couldn't climb on top of her table never mind a roof top. And the couple at 26 and the young man at 28 were all clearly innocent. But at 29 we struck gold.

'No one of that name here,' the young woman said.

'A tall man, dark hair, American accent?' Bob persisted.

Her eyes widened. 'Ah! You have the number the wrong way round! Not 27, it's 72. And he's not American, he's Canadian. My cleaner works for him too. Says he's a nice quiet gentleman. Sleeps most of the day and seems to work nights.'

'His name?'

She frowned. 'Delaney. Yes, that's it, Robert Delaney!'

As she closed the door Bob Fabian turned to me. 'This time . . . this time we have our man!'

The squad joined us and we moved in on Delaney's flat. The chief inspector gave Bob Fabian the honour of arresting him, while I had the honour of snapping the handcuffs on the Cat's Burglar's powerful wrists.

Robert Augustus Delaney went to prison for three years.

Bob Fabian went on to become one of the most brilliant detectives the Flying Squad has ever seen. I learned a lot from him in the years I worked with him.

But I'd made that stupid mistake at first. I'd believed that good detection was all about following clues and solving mysteries. That's not the *whole* truth.

Good detection is mostly about patience and hard work. Long hours of watching and waiting. Long miles of walking the streets and asking questions.

Bob knew that. I didn't. That was my mistake.

FACT FILE

The Flying Squad— FACT FILE

Sometimes police forces set up special detective squads to catch particular types of criminal. One of the most famous is the British Police Force's 'Flying Squad'.

1. The Flying Squad was formed in 1919. It began with just twelve detectives and two horse-drawn wagons. Now it has over 200 detectives and some of the fastest cars on Britain's roads.

2. The Flying Squad officers get a lot of valuable information by pretending

to be friendly with criminals. In 1944 a new section of the Flying Squad was set up. A group of just four or five officers had to mix in the criminal 'underworld', but not be seen as police officers. They had to be practically 'invisible' as they gathered information. They were told to be as invisible as ghosts. They were known as 'The Ghost Squad'. In 1944 they made more arrests than any other Flying Squad officers.

3. The Ghost Squad made good use of informers— criminals who were paid to tell the police who had committed certain crimes or who was planning a crime. Informers worked in secret. The criminals could kill them if they found out who was betraying them, so the Ghost Squad's informers used code names. Some curious ones

included Slicer Fred, Stir-happy Lou and Bert the Lorry.

4. Londoners used rhyming slang to give the Flying Squad its nickname, The Sweeney. This is short for Sweeney Todd. Todd was a famous character in Victorian stories, a barber who murdered his customers and had them made into meat pies. A television series was made in the 1970s about the Flying Squad. It was called *The Sweeney*.

5. Working too closely with the underworld has its problems. In the 1970s some officers became too friendly with the criminals and began to take bribes. In return they let the crooks get away with some of their crimes. The Flying Squad officers were eventually caught and sent to

prison.

The Flying Squad officers were not the only ones to cross the line from solving crimes to committing crimes.

THE PERFECT CRIME

There's an old saying, 'Set a thief to catch a thief.' Thieves are experts in crime, so they should be able to detect the work of other criminals. But the darker side of this is 'Set a law man to beat a law man'—a policeman should make an excellent criminal because he knows how the enemy works.

England, 1989

The man slipped a plastic card into the cash machine, punched in some numbers, and a few minutes later walked away with a handful of cash.

The street was quiet at that time of night. No one saw him get back into his car and drive away. No one heard him chuckle to himself, 'The perfect crime!'

*   *   *

'It's the perfect crime,' Martin Evans groaned and shook his head. He looked too young to be a policeman, but he was. He almost looked too young to be sitting in that smoky pub sipping a pint of beer.

Rod Whitchelo rested his elbows on the table and looked at the young detective. 'I always thought there was such a thing as a perfect crime. I even thought of writing a book about it when I left the police force.'

'You did?' Detective Constable Evans said. He enjoyed these chats with Rod Whitchelo after work each evening. Rod had a lot of experience and gave him tips on some of his cases.

'Yeah. So tell me again about this one. I might be able to use some tips,' Whitchelo grinned. He was a heavy man and his strong hands gripped the beer glass.

Martin Evans sat back. 'This criminal has been planning it for a long time. First he opened a bank account two years ago—so long ago that no one in the bank can remember what he looks like. Then he sent a letter to the director of a pet-food company. In the letter he said he would poison cans of dog food on supermarket shelves across the country. Once dog owners found out about it they would stop buying that dog food and the company

113

would lose millions of pounds. All the criminal wanted was £100,000.'

'Extortion. It's an easy way to make money,' Rod Whitchelo commented.

'But we always catch blackmailers like that. It's like kidnappers. There's one weak spot in any plan: that's the moment when the criminal picks up the cash. We can mark the bank notes, put a tracking device in the container and surround the area with plain-clothes observers. That's why it's such a rare crime in Britain. They know they can't get away with it!' the young detective said.

'But this pet-food poisoner found a way round that?' Whitchelo said slowly.

'Yes. He asked the company to pay money into his bank account—the one he opened two years ago. He can go to any cash-dispensing machine and draw out a couple of hundred pounds every day. But there are nine hundred of his bank's cash tills around the country. He can draw money from any one of them. *Nine hundred!* He can visit one at any time. There's no chance of him getting caught.'

'So the pet-food company paid?' Whitchelo asked.

'We advised them to go along with the plan while we worked on catching the man,' Martin Evans said.

'What were you looking for?'

'A pattern. We wanted to see where he drew the money out. We could watch the cash machine and catch him,' the young detective said. 'Of course he was too clever for that. He drew the money out all over the country—Wales one day, Scotland the next. All we could do was wait for him to make a mistake.'

'He sounds too clever to make a mistake,' Whitchelo shrugged.

'But he has!' Martin cried, and his eyes glowed with triumph. 'He got greedy! He threatened to put razor blades in baby food. Asked for another £100,000 to stop.'

'That's not exactly greedy,' Whitchelo argued. 'Those food manufacturers make millions of pounds. And it's hardly a *mistake*.'

'Oh, but it *is*!' the detective constable

said. 'It's one thing threatening to kill a dog. But threatening to kill babies is another matter. That brings in Scotland Yard and all the police forces in the country. Our Regional Crime Squad has been struggling to find time to investigate this case. Now we have the help of every police force in the country. We had ten officers on the dog-food case, but we'll have three thousand on the baby food.'

Whitchelo sipped his beer thoughtfully. 'I still don't see how that will help.'

'It means Chief Superintendent Fleming of Scotland Yard can have each of those nine hundred cash tills watched by three men: one inside the bank reading the cash card number and two outside waiting to grab him. He won't get away this time!'

*   *   *

Chief Superintendent Fleming paced up and down the office. He was angry. 'How did he know? We had three men watching each machine—three thousand men in all. We couldn't miss him. So, what does our blackmailer do? He stops using the machines.'

Detective Superintendent Leacey shuffled papers on his desk and pulled out a sheet. He ran a finger down the columns of figures. 'You're right, sir. He drew money out every day for three weeks. On the three nights we watched the cash points he didn't draw one penny. He must have spotted one of our watchers.'

'He shouldn't have. They're professionals,' the Scotland Yard man snapped.

'Maybe he's a professional too,' Leacey began to say when the phone on his desk rang. 'Excuse me, sir,' he said as he picked up the receiver. After a minute he put the phone down and looked up at the chief superintendent. 'Well, sir, we have some good news and some bad news.'

'Get on with it, Leacey,' Fleming said.

'Our friend has drawn money out of a cash till in Ipswich.'

The chief superintendent muttered a

curse. 'On the first night we stop watching the machines? That's too lucky to be coincidence; he must be getting inside information.' He ran a hand through his short grey hair and began pacing again. 'So what's the good news?'

'It seems the Ipswich branch is one where there are cameras in place— video cameras. We should be able to see his face.'

Fleming stopped walking and gave a grim smile. 'His first mistake, Leacey?'

'Could be, sir. A squad car has brought the video to our lecture room. Would you like to see it?'

'Would a drowning man like to see a lifebelt? Show me the way!'

But half an hour later Chief Superintendent Fleming's face was set in a scowl, making the deep lines on his face deeper and the pale, set lips thinner and harder. He stared at the image on the television screen. A man was collecting money from a cash point at a bank. Fleming could see he was tall and heavily built, but the man had cleverly placed a motorcycle crash

helmet over his head. There was a smoked glass visor in front of his face.

'The picture's as much use as one of the Invisible Man,' the detective from Scotland Yard said. 'He knows every trick we have up our sleeves. He knew *when* we were watching and now he knows *how* we're watching.'

'So what do we do, sir?' Leacey asked.

Fleming looked at him tiredly. 'We give up, Leacey. We give up.'

*   *   *

'We've given up,' young Martin Evans

said in the pub. Rod Whitchelo looked into his beer and watched the bubbles drift lazily to the surface and disappear. 'I suppose I can't write that book about the perfect crime, can I? It's so perfect that everyone would want to try it. The police would never let me publish it.'

The young detective constable nodded unhappily. 'And we don't want any more accidents. He's putting pressure on for more money now. He's actually poisoned some jars of baby food and put razor blades in others. It's vicious, but what can we do except pay up?'

'He put warnings into the jars, didn't he?' Whitchelo asked. 'At least that's what it said on the television.'

'Hah! He put a strip of metal label with a warning printed on it. Of course it sank to the bottom of the jar. The mother only found the label *after* she'd fed the baby. By then the poor child was spitting blood. Vicious!' Martin Evans repeated. 'And of course now it's become public there are lots of loonies trying to copy the blackmailer. You wouldn't believe what they've been putting in food—drawing pins, glass, fuse wire . . . Mind you, some phone the supermarket and lie about poisoning the food just to try to make a bit of money. They all get caught.'

'Not as clever as the original then?' Whitchelo asked.

'You sound as if you admire the man,' the young detective said bitterly.

The man held up a large hand. 'I wouldn't say that. But you have to admit he has a good brain.'

'He's got a twisted brain, Rod. And I only wish we could have caught him.'

*   *   *

Chief Superintendent Fleming loosened his tie. The room was pretty full and getting hotter. He called out, 'Can I have your attention, please?'

The men and women turned towards him and looked at him curiously. 'Some of you may know that I am Chief Superintendent Fleming of Scotland Yard. I'm in charge of the baby-food blackmail case. You probably also know that the police haven't had a great deal of success in nailing the villain.'

There was a mumble of agreement from Fleming's audience. 'That's why we're bringing you lot in from Special Branch. It's not simply that the ordinary Regional Crime Squads have failed. It's that we suspect he's getting information directly from police sources. In Special Branch you don't usually mix with regional squad officers. The operation you are involved with will be codenamed "Agincourt" and it's *top secret*.'

The chief superintendent gave a detailed description of the case so far. 'Any questions?' he finished.

A woman in the second row raised a hand. 'I'm DC Susan Digby, sir. How are you planning to catch him this time? I mean, in Special Branch we don't have three thousand officers, do we?'

'No, Susan, but our villainous friend is getting careless now. It seems word has got back to him that we're giving up on the chase. That's exactly what I wanted him to think. He believes he doesn't need to travel the country to make money. He's sticking to London now. We'll watch the main London cash machines on the 20th and 21st of October and hopefully get him that way.'

'But what are we looking for?' Susan Digby persisted.

Fleming looked around the room at fifty pairs of knowing eyes. 'Anything suspicious. You're all experienced officers. Police routine hasn't worked so far, so now we'll try a bit of Special Branch intelligence. I don't know *exactly* what you're looking for, but I trust you'll know it when you see it.' He stacked his sheets of notes neatly and slipped them into a folder marked 'Agincourt'. 'If there are no more questions then I'll leave your chief superintendent to organize the details . . . and the best of luck!'

* * *

Luck was with Fleming's team that night. A careless workman cut through a computer cable operating the cash point at Uxbridge, just outside London—a machine that was *not* being watched by Special Branch. That was the machine the blackmailer chose that night.

The man stared at the small green and black screen. 'Sorry, this machine is out of service. The nearest cash point is in Enfield. We apologize for any inconvenience.'

The man sighed and walked back to his car.

As he pulled up outside the Enfield office his luck finally ran out. Susan Digby and a Special Branch colleague were sitting in a car across the road. They watched as the man stepped out of the car.

Susan felt a cold slug of excitement creeping up her back. 'That's him,' she said. 'Wait till he's taken the money, then we'll arrest him.'

The officers slipped quietly out of their car and waited in the shadow of a shop doorway until the man turned back to his car. As he reached for the door handle Susan stepped forward briskly and laid a hand on his arm. 'Excuse me, sir, we are police officers,' and she flipped open her ID.

'What do you want?' the man said. 'I've done nothing wrong.'

'We were wondering why you're wearing a crash helmet when you're driving a car,' she said.

'In case I get wet,' the man said and tried to laugh, but the sound died in his throat.

'I am arresting you on suspicion of blackmail,' she said. 'Would you mind telling me your name, sir?'

The man tugged the helmet off and rested it tiredly on the roof of the car. 'Whitchelo. Rodney Whitchelo.'

'Occupation?'

'Retired. Retired policeman,' he said.

*   *   *

Martin Evans supped his beer miserable and alone in the pub. The barman wiped the table and said, 'Your friend Rod not coming in tonight?'

'No,' the young policeman said. 'Not

125

tonight . . . and not for a very long time, I'd say.'

'Problems?'

'He thought he'd discovered the perfect crime,' Martin said.

'But he hadn't?'

'There's no such thing.'

FACT FILE

Changing sides—
FACT FILE

1. Whitchelo pleaded 'Not guilty' to the charges but the jury found him guilty and the judge sentenced him to seventeen years in prison. Officers searching his flat found the typewriter on which the blackmail note had been written and some of the poison that had been placed in jars. One of Whitchelo's tricks was to phone friends and say he was at home so that he had an 'alibi' for the times when cash was being collected hundreds of miles away. Police found his mobile phone. The calls from it

were traced and they matched the places where the money had been collected. They also found tapes of Whitchelo's attempts to write his book on the perfect crime. One piece of advice was 'Don't get greedy'. He'd already made almost £20,000 from his scheme when he was caught. If he'd stopped then he might never have been detected. It was his greed for more and more that finally led to his downfall.

2. Food manufacturers now make their jars safe by sealing them with clear plastic. No one can poison a glass jar without breaking the seal and giving the secret away. Whitchelo's 'perfect crime' is no longer possible.

3. It's not only policemen who are tempted to break the

128

laws they are supposed to enforce. Sir Jonah Barrington was an Irish judge. When he needed money he stole it from his court. Sir Jonah got away with it for twenty years before he was eventually caught in 1830 and sent for trial in his own court.

4. Fifty years later in the USA, Roy Bean was a gambler, saloon-keeper and smuggler before he found the best job of all—as a judge! Trials were often held up while 'Judge' Bean drank whisky or played cards with his friends. He made up laws to suit himself, found people guilty and fined them, then put the fines straight into his own pocket!

5. Henry Morgan was much more successful. He was a pirate who raided Spanish colonies in South America.

In 1672 he was called to England to explain his crimes. He explained himself so well that he was knighted and became Sir Henry. Then he was sent back to the West Indies as the Governor of Jamaica. He had the job of detecting and punishing pirates in the region. That was quite easy for Morgan— they were his old friends. He arrested them and had them executed.

THE JEWEL THIEVES

When the police have a suspect they use 'interrogation' questioning—to try to find the truth. Professional criminals are often skilled in lying and interrogation can fail. The police have to stick to the interrogation rules: they can't beat or torture a suspect, they can't invent evidence or tell lies. But sometimes they try one or two tricks of their own to get the proof they need, especially if they belong to the Canadian police and have the reputation for 'always getting their man . . .'

Toronto, Canada, 1956

'I know they're guilty,' Detective Inspector Jim Collins sighed. 'We *all* know they're guilty. Proving it's another thing.'

'Tell me what you've got and I'll see if I can help,' his superintendent said. 'You're holding two men on suspicion of the jewellery store thefts, is that right?'

'Right. We've been chasing them for five weeks,' Jim Collins said and sat forward in the chair. 'It seemed they

132

were really very professional. The two men walked into the jewellers' shops and asked to see the best necklaces. The assistants took them out of the display cases and started talking about them. Of course they were so keen to sell the jewels they didn't pay enough attention to what else was going on in the shop.'

'The woman?'

'That's right. A blonde woman came into the shop with them, and while the men were talking she pretended to be looking around. In fact she was stealing something pretty valuable from the cases or the window display. Why, in one shop she even disconnected an alarm before she opened a case! Of course the shops didn't discover the thefts for quite some time, sometimes not till the next day,' the detective said, punching the palm of his hand in irritation.

'And you had nothing to go on?' the superintendent asked.

'Descriptions. We knew one man was very thin and the other was stocky with his hair combed forward to cover his bald spot. We nicknamed them Laurel and Hardy.'

The superintendent chuckled. 'You showed the shop assistants photos of some of the Toronto jewel thieves?'

'Oh, yes. But Laurel and Hardy and their girlfriend are from out of town. It seemed we'd never catch them until we had a bit of good luck. A thin man and a blonde woman were arrested for suspected shoplifting in a town-centre store. We couldn't make the charge stick and we had to let them go, but . . . I'm not sure if I should be telling you this, sir,' Collins said, tugging awkwardly at his shirt cuff.

'I can always pretend I didn't hear it,' his senior officer said.

'One of the arresting officers found a photograph of the man and woman in a pocket when they were searched. He accidentally forgot to return it to Mr Laurel when the couple were released.'

'An easy mistake to make,' the superintendent said with an innocent face. 'You showed the photograph to the jewellery shop assistants?'

'And they confirmed that they were

134

the suspects. Of course we now knew who the thieves were but we had absolutely no proof. No one saw them steal the jewels, no jewels were found in their possession, and no fingerprints were left on the jewellery cases,' Collins said.

'But we were able to keep a lookout for them?'

'We were. The jewellers weren't so careful. Two more thefts were reported last Friday. That's when a patrol-car driver spotted Laurel and Hardy in a grey Ford driving down the High Street. He pulled them in. They denied any knowledge about jewels and they certainly had nothing on them.'

'You searched their apartment?' the senior officer asked.

'They refused to tell us where they lived. But we had two clues: a collection of three keys in Laurel's pocket and a scrap of paper that said "Hotel Room 400" with an almost invisible phone number. While Forensic worked on tracing the hotel from the phone number we looked at the car. There was a parking ticket inside dated two nights before. We went down to the street where the ticket was issued.'

'What were you looking for?' the superintendent asked. 'A needle in a haystack?'

Inspector Collins couldn't help but looked pleased with himself. 'A door that fitted Laurel's key,' he said.

'Bit of a long shot, surely?'

'But it worked. We found a block of rented rooms that it fitted. The caretaker recognized the photograph of Laurel and we found a gun in the man's room—an illegal gun. At last we had a reason to keep him in prison while we look into the jewel thefts.'

'But no jewels?'

'No jewels. I said these guys were professionals. They wouldn't leave them where we could find them. Then we traced the hotel where Hardy was staying, and what did we find there?'

'Nothing?'

'Nothing. No jewels and no blonde. She must have them with her. We wheeled Hardy in and held two identity parades. The jewellers picked out

Laurel and Hardy every time.'

The superintendent walked across the room and poured out two cups of coffee from a percolator on the table. As he handed one to Jim Collins he said, 'I see your problem. It would never stand up in court. All you can prove is that Laurel and Hardy were in the shops. There's nothing to prove that they stole anything. A good lawyer would have the case thrown out of court. No, Jim, you need the jewels.'

'We've questioned them for twelve hours now. They're saying nothing. We'll have to let them go tomorrow morning. All that work and they're laughing at us.'

'You questioned them separately?' the superintendent said as he sipped at the scalding black coffee.

'Of course. We haven't let them talk to each other since they were arrested. We don't want to give them the chance to compare stories. We keep hoping they'll slip up, make a mistake. But . . .'

'But they're professionals,' the superintendent finished. He looked over the rim of his cup and remarked,

'Perhaps it's time we stopped being so professional ourselves.'

'I don't understand, sir,' Jim Collins said.

'Perhaps we should get careless. Let them have a couple of cells next door to each other. When they see how careless we can be, then maybe *they'll* get a little careless. Maybe they'll talk.'

Jim Collins looked into the dark steaming liquid and tried to picture it. 'There are two cells below the interview rooms. There's a third cell across the passage from them. Somebody in that third cell could hear everything they say.'

'So, try it,' the superintendent said.

The detective rose slowly to his feet and drained his coffee. 'It hardly seems fair, sir.'

'There's no law against listening to two villains having a chat, but there is a very definite law against stealing thousands of pounds' worth of jewellery. You joined the police force to stop them . . . by hook or by crook. So do it.'

* * *

The man they called Laurel looked nothing like the old film comedian. This man was taller and his eyes were harder. His mouth was unsmiling, yet something about his face showed satisfaction. 'They won't hold us,' he said.

The man in the next cell had small, shifting eyes buried in a fat face. 'What about the gun charge?'

'We'll be given bail. We'll have a hearing tomorrow morning and it's a minor offence. They don't know about our past record in Ontario. They'll ask for a couple of hundred dollars and let us go.'

'And do you want us to jump bail?' the fat one asked.

'Better lose a couple of hundred dollars than let them find the jewels and lock us away for ten years!'

'So you reckon they won't find the jewels? Where are they anyway?'

The hoarse voice of the fat man echoed down the concrete row of cells. In one cell across the corridor a policeman with a notebook held his breath and waited for the answer.

'In the next block. Separated by a steel wall,' the thin one replied.

Perhaps it was the soft rustle of the policeman's notebook that unsettled the man. 'I wonder why they put us together in these cells. You don't suppose they're bugged, do you?'

The fat man rolled his little eyes nervously round the cell, looking for a microphone. 'Nah!' he said. 'They'd never think of anything as smart as that.'

Detective Inspector Collins yawned. It had been a long night but he had to find those jewels before morning. The court would free the crooks and they'd vanish. The shops would lose a fortune in jewellery . . . and the Canadian police would have a black mark against them in the minds of the shopkeepers.

He stepped into the hotel to meet the manager. The man was wearing a dressing gown and his hair had a slept-in look. 'Sorry to trouble you at this time of night,' Collins said.

'It's morning. Three a.m. to be exact,' the manager said sourly.

'Yes. You were kind enough to let us search the suspect's room this afternoon,' the detective said.

'No problem. But you found nothing, did you?'

'We didn't. But we have reason to believe that the jewels may be hidden behind a steel wall. Would you know where that is?'

The manager rubbed a hand over his unshaven chin. 'The whole block is divided into two by a steel wall,' he explained. 'Fire regulations. There's a steel wall at the end of each corridor.'

'At the end of the suspect's corridor?'

'Of course.'

'So, what's on the other side of the steel wall?'

The manager looked impatient. 'The other half of the corridor, of course. And another block of rooms.'

'So how could he hide something there?' Jim Collins asked.

'He couldn't. Unless he'd booked another room,' the manager suggested.

'Did he?'

'No. The man booked Room 400, the one you searched.'

'Did the man or the woman go into the other half of the building for any reason?' the detective asked desperately.

Now the manager said something which stopped the inspector's heart for half a beat. He said, 'What woman?'

Jim Collins was wide awake now. 'The suspect booked Room 400. He had a blonde woman with him.'

'No, he didn't,' the manager said.

The detective slid a hand inside his jacket pocket and was pleased he'd remembered to bring the photograph with him. 'So you've never seen this woman?'

'Sure I've seen that woman,' the manager said.

'You told me she wasn't with the man in Room 400!' Jim Collins cried.

'She wasn't. She came in yesterday and took a room in the other half of the building. Room 207, I think.'

The detective cursed himself. 'Why didn't you tell me the suspect was alone?'

'You never asked!' the angry manager replied.

'Sorry! Sorry!' Jim Collins said. 'Could we go to Room 207 now?'

'She'll be asleep,' the manager objected.

'Shame,' the detective snapped.

*   *   *

After the blonde woman had been wakened and hurried off to the police

143

station for questioning, the team of detectives got to work. 'These crooks are professionals,' Jim Collins told his men.

'So are we, sir,' one of his men assured him. 'If a piece of gold has rested in this room we'll find its shadow.'

Jim Collins sank tiredly against the door post and let them carry out the search. The curtains were pulled open and the pearl-grey light of early morning spilled into the room. There wasn't much time left.

But when the searchers reached the couch under the window they struck gold . . . and diamond and platinum. Ten rings and a $5,000 watch were enough for the inspector to start with.

He drove through the empty streets too quickly and arrived as the manager of Howard's Credit Jewellers was having breakfast. 'Can you identify any of these as your property?' he asked.

The manager could. Collins gave him just ten minutes to shave and dress. The man was still chewing toast as they raced towards the courtroom.

The unsmiling man whom the

144

detectives called Laurel sat in the dock of the courtroom. That faint expression of confidence was on his face. It was still there when Inspector Jim Collins stepped into the witness box and faced the court's questions.

'And have you recovered any of the jewellery, Inspector?' the judge asked.

Jim Collins looked at the crooks and it was his turn to smile. 'Yes, your honour. We have a stolen watch and ten rings.'

The judge looked at the defendants. 'I believe you have a case to answer. You will go on trial for the theft of jewellery. No bail.'

As Detective Inspector Collins wandered out of the courtroom he was greeted by his superintendent. 'Coffee?'

'I'd rather have a few hours' sleep,' he groaned.

'So our plan worked?'

'Yes, sir.'

'Who was it said "Cheats never beats"?'

'I don't know, sir . . . but they were wrong.'

145

FACT FILE

Criminal records—
FACT FILE

1.   The thieves known to Collins as 'Laurel and Hardy' were sentenced to six years in jail each. Two years later a jewellery shop assistant reported a theft and described a suspicious character who had been hanging around that day. It happened that Collins was asked to deal with the case. 'Sounds just like a guy we jailed two years ago,' he said. 'But he's in jail.' He checked anyway. 'Laurel' had been released early for good conduct ... and gone straight back to the shoplifting racket. His bad luck in being

matched against Collins again meant he went back to prison for the remaining four years.

2. Normally the police would hope to trace someone who repeats a crime from their records. Every time an arrest is made the criminal has his or her fingerprints and photograph taken. Some police forces then add details of the people they commit crimes with (their 'associates') and the skills the criminal has.

3. Police may also keep examples of a criminal's handwriting. In a 1956 American kidnap case the criminal was trapped with the help of police records. Police passed on his ransom note to handwriting experts. They checked all written confessions in the files, reading more than a million samples over six weeks, but in the end

148

they found the one that matched.

4. Modern science can identify individuals from their voice. A criminal's 'voice-print' can be taken, printed and stored like a fingerprint. Even if a person tried to disguise their voice, the voice-print can recognize it. This is very useful for police checking telephone calls which are threatening or which are made by a kidnapper demanding a ransom. There is an interesting case of voice-testing in the Bible, thousands of years before electronic voice-prints. The leader Jephthah wanted to detect the enemy Ephraimites in his group of followers. He asked everyone to say the word 'Shibboleth'. The Ephraimites pronounced it 'Sibboleth' (without the 'h'). Jephthah's detective work was a success!

5. Samples of a criminal's blood can now be taken and matched to any tiny scrap of hair, blood or skin left at the scene of a crime. This is know as 'DNA printing' and is said by some scientists to be as reliable as a fingerprint, though twins will have the same DNA print. Unfortunately mistakes can be made by testers. At least one man had his life ruined with a prison sentence where the only evidence against him was a faulty DNA test. Yet in 1994 the law in Britain was changed to allow police to keep DNA test records of criminals.

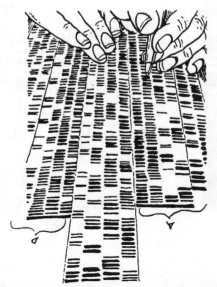

THE GHOSTLY DETECTIVE

Sometimes the best detective in the world can fail to solve a crime, then the solution comes in a strange and unexpected way. It is almost as if the victim of the crime has returned from the grave to provide the final clue.

Kent, England, 1922

'I've a strange story to tell,' the old man said. He was shrunken and grey inside a worn black suit but there was a fierce intelligence in the sad, shadowed eyes.

Superintendent Edward Carlin was too busy to listen to strange stories. 'I know you're busy,' the old man said, as if he could read the policeman's mind, 'but I will try to keep my story brief.'

The superintendent relaxed and invited the man to take the battered armchair while he sat down again behind an office desk littered with papers, files and forms.

'My name is George Tombe,' the old man began, 'and I am the vicar of a small church in Sydenham. I live there with my wife, Victoria, and we have a

152

son, Eric. At least,' he said, looking away from the policeman to hide some sudden pain, 'we *had* a son called Eric. Victoria and I have every reason to believe we will never see him again.'

'Perhaps the "Missing Persons" register at your regional police headquarters would be able to help you, Reverend Tombe,' the policeman said.

'Ah, no. We have no hope of finding Eric alive, you understand. We believe he is dead. It is simply our wish that we may find his body and give it a Christian burial. I have come to Scotland Yard because our local police said that you have the sort of information I may need.'

'We have crime records, Reverend. Are you suggesting your son is the victim of a crime?'

'Precisely,' the old man said with a curious bow of the head. 'I have done all the detective work that I can possibly do, but I lack your contacts . . . and your experience, of course. I am coming to you as a last resort.'

'Tell me what you have found,' Superintendent Carlin said, 'and I'll see if we can help.'

'Thank you, Superintendent,' the vicar said, opening the black leather briefcase on his knee. 'This is the last letter we received from Eric,' he said as he passed the note across the desk.

'Dated Tuesday the seventeenth of April last year,' the policeman read. *'I shall be coming to see you on Saturday.'* He looked up. 'He never arrived?'

'He never arrived. His flat in the West End of London was deserted. It seemed he had vanished without taking any clothes. We placed adverts in local and national newspapers, but there was no response. We informed the local police but they said, as no doubt you would say, that hundreds of people go missing every year and that most of them turn up after a couple of months.'

'They sent enquiries to hospitals and searched accident records, did they?' Carlin asked.

Again the vicar bowed his head. 'They did indeed. I have no complaints on that score. They did what they could. They could not, however, spare the time to search for my son. I knew

154

I'd have to do that myself.'

Superintendent Carlin had to admire the vicar as the old man told his story of the search for his son Eric. He'd arrived in London and begun by knocking on the doors of his son's neighbours. The neighbours all confirmed that Eric had been missing since about April and one or two were able to give him the names of people his son had known.

For three months the old man trailed the streets of London, riding nervously on new motor buses or being rattled through dingy tunnels on underground trains. But each journey ended in the same way, at a dead end.

Every weekend he would return to his parish in Sydenham and report back to Victoria. Every weekend he would have to watch her disappointed face as he told of his failure to track down their son. 'Perhaps you should stop now. You are wearing yourself out,' she would say.

'One more try,' he would insist. 'One more try.'

That last Monday morning he

decided to talk to the barber who cut Eric's hair. Barbers are chatty people. If he remembered Eric then he might remember him talking about his plans.

'We talked about the war, sir,' the barber told the old man. 'And after the war I understand Mister Eric went into the motor trade. I believe he had some money in the bank, which he invested in two garages.'

'Do you remember where they were?'

'No, sir. But I understand they did not succeed. From what Mister Eric said, I think his partner was as much to blame as anything. He was not a very sound businessman.'

'And do you remember the name of this partner?' the vicar asked eagerly.

'Afraid not, sir . . . though he did come here once.'

'He came *here*? That's a coincidence,' the vicar said.

'Not at all, sir. Mister Eric recommended us to the gentleman. We put that sort of introduction in our little reference book, sir.'

'And could I see this book?' the

Reverend Tombe asked.

'Here we are, sir,' the barber said, opening the small red book. 'Ernest Dyer's the name. His address is "The Welcomes", Kenley . . . and it says here, "Introduced by Mr Eric Tombe."'

Superintendent Carlin interrupted the old man's story at this point. 'Dyer, you say? That name's familiar. Excuse me a moment.' He picked up the telephone on his desk and dialled. 'Edmonds? I think we have a file on someone called Dyer, don't we? Ernest Dyer. Can you bring it to my office?' He replaced the phone on its cradle and said, 'Sorry, Reverend. Carry on.'

The vicar had visited 'The Welcomes' the next day. The bleak and blackened skeleton of a farmhouse stood in a shabby yard. The whole place had a gloomy and neglected air about it. A woman came from the stable block to meet him. 'I'm looking for an Ernest Dyer,' he said, raising his hat.

'Aren't we all!' the woman said sourly. 'I'm his wife. He disappeared

157

some time last month. He owes a lot of people a lot of money. I suppose you're after some yourself, are you?'

'No, no. I am trying to trace my son, Eric Tombe,' the old man explained.

The woman softened a little. 'Ah, you're Eric's father, are you? Come into the stables and I'll try to help you.'

'The stables?'

'That's where we live now, since the house burned down.'

'How unfortunate.'

'Hah! Unfortunate!' she snorted as she led the way towards the block of stone buildings. 'Another one of Ernest's little plans that went wrong. We bought that house for £5,000 and Ernest insured it for £12,000. When it burned down the insurance company refused to pay.'

'Why was that?'

'The insurance inspector spotted one or two petrol cans lying around and accused Ernest of burning his own house down. Ernest didn't argue.'

'Oh, dear!' the vicar said, worrying about the man his son had been mixed up with.

'Look, I have to be honest, Mr Tombe; I haven't seen your Eric since Easter. You knew he had a big row with Ernest, did you?'

'No, I didn't.'

'Eric accused Ernest of forging his signature on some of their business cheques. Knowing Ernest, that was probably true. Ernest and Eric went away after that. They split the partnership and I haven't seen them since. Maybe the bank will have some record of your son, Mr Tombe,' she suggested.

'Do you have their address?' he asked.

Mrs Dyer found a letter from the manager and the Reverend Tombe copied it down. 'And you have no idea where Eric went?' he asked.

'Ernest showed me a telegram from Eric. It said "Have been called overseas." Does that help?'

The vicar frowned. 'No. I'm sorry, Mrs Dyer, but Eric never used the word "overseas" in his life. I don't want to call your husband a liar . . .'

'Why not? Everyone else does.'

'I just can't believe that Eric sent

that telegram.'

'Can't say I blame you,' the woman agreed.

There didn't seem much else she could tell him. The old man crossed the icy mud of the farmyard and set off down the track to the village. He reached the bank before it closed that day.

The bank manager was dressed in a smart black tail coat and was smooth as the bank's marble floor. 'No need to worry, Mr Tombe. We had a letter from your son just a month or so ago.'

'May I see it?'

'It is not normal practice . . . but I suppose there is no harm, if it will set your mind at rest,' the manager smiled. He slid the letter across to the vicar.

The Reverend Tombe looked up. 'I'm sorry,' he said, 'very sorry. But this letter is not from my son. It is not his handwriting or his signature.'

'But it asks for all his money to be transferred to Mr Ernest Dyer,' the manager gasped. 'Mr Dyer has since emptied the account. If this letter is a forgery, then Dyer has robbed your son!'

The old man said simply, 'I fear he

160

may have done more than simply robbed him.'

*　　*　　*

Superintendent Carlin studied the file for a few minutes, then said, 'It's not good news, Reverend. The Yorkshire police had a report of a man who was attempting a business fraud in Scarborough. Detective Inspector Abbot went to investigate and met the man in a hotel. The man offered to go to his room to settle the matter, but on the way upstairs he reached inside his jacket pocket. Abbot thought he was trying to destroy some evidence. He grabbed the man and they struggled. In the struggle Abbot discovered that the suspect was in fact reaching for a gun. The gun went off accidentally and the suspect died instantly.'

'That man was Ernest Dyer?'

'He was. When the inspector searched the room he found a passport in the name of Eric Tombe . . . and a hundred cheques with Tombe's signature on them,' the Superintendent

161

said, studying his file. 'At the time the Yorkshire police made no attempt to trace this Eric Tombe. They thought that he was just an invention of Dyer's—a secret identity if he ever needed to escape to the continent.' He looked up from the reports. 'This seems to confirm your worst fears, Reverend.'

'Indeed,' the old man sighed. 'Dyer is—or was—a killer. He had argued with my son over the cheques and no doubt killed him. Then he began forging Eric's signature on bank letters and cheques in order to continue taking my son's money.'

'That seems a likely course of events,' the policeman agreed. 'You have done a magnificent job of piecing together your son's story, Reverend, a wonderful piece of detective work. My own men couldn't have done better. It's only a pity that Dyer's death means we may never find what you want— your son's body.'

Then the old man said something. He spoke so matter-of-factly that Superintendent Carlin wondered if

162

he'd heard him correctly. 'What did you say?'

'I said, we *know* where Eric's body is. We simply need your help in uncovering it.'

'Then why—'

'I hadn't quite finished my story, Superintendent. I returned home from the bank with the news about Eric. My wife and I talked it over for a long time and we persuaded ourselves that he must be dead. But then Victoria began to have dreams—the strangest and most horrifying dreams. And in these dreams she saw Eric's body. It was lying at the bottom of a well. At first I thought it was just a nightmare, but night after night the dream returned. I believe it is not a dream but a message from the afterlife, Superintendent. No, I don't expect you to believe in such nonsense, but just in case there is something in it, could I ask you to investigate the possibility?'

Just twice in his life Superintendent Carlin was lost for words. The first time was when Reverend Tombe told his story of the dream. The second was

163

when he drove down to "The Welcomes" to question Mrs Dyer about Eric Tombe's disappearance. She couldn't tell him much more than she had told the vicar.

'One final question, Mrs Dyer,' the policeman said as he was folding away his notebook. 'Would you have such a thing as a well on your farm?'

The woman shrugged. 'A disused well, Superintendent. There are five on our land. Do you think Ernest hid something there? It wouldn't surprise me. Now you mention it, I was alone in the farm one night when I heard stones being dropped down the well behind the barn. When I went outside with the dog I saw a man in the shadows.'

'Who was it, Mrs Dyer?'

'It was my husband. He told me not to come near, but he never did explain what he was doing that night.'

'If you don't mind, Mrs Dyer, we'll search that well,' the policeman said.

*   *   *

'Dust to dust and ashes to ashes,' the

164

Reverend said. 'I have buried many people in my time as a vicar. I never thought I'd see the day when I'd have to bury poor Eric.'

'At least you found him, sir. You and your wife and that remarkable dream,' Superintendent Carlin said in the cool calm of the church after the service.

The old man dabbed at the tears that were running down his face. 'No, Superintendent. He was found for us by someone far greater than Victoria or me, someone that we'll have to meet one day. As the poet William Cowper said, "God moves in a mysterious way, His wonders to perform."'

EPILOGUE

The stories in this book are all about unusual cases of detective work, cases where the investigator had to solve a puzzle to clear up a crime. That's what many people think of when they picture detective work, but most detectives will tell you that patience, persistence and the ability to ask the right questions are just as important as solving puzzles.

In the last two hundred years science has been helping the detective more and more. Unfortunately, criminals soon learn about science. The scientist discovers fingerprinting, the detective discovers a use for it in crimefighting, and the criminal discovers a use for gloves! The scientist invents the video camera, the detective discovers its use in keeping an electronic eye on valuables, and the criminal discovers a new use for a mask! And so it goes on.

But it's not all a losing battle for the detective. Criminals have been bringing misery to their victims for thousands of years, yet the oldest aid to detection is still one of the best—the witness. Two-thirds of solved crimes are unravelled with the help of a witness—someone like you. Police can't be everywhere all of the time, so they rely on the public informing them of unusual or suspicious happenings.

You can be the detective's best friend. In the world of true detective stories, you are one of the main characters.